Grasshopper Falls

Books by Merrill Gilfillan

Truck. Poems. Angel Hair Books, New York, 1970.

9:15. Poems. Doones Press, Bowling Green, Ohio, 1970.

To Creature. Poems. Blue Wind Press, Berkeley, 1975.

Light Years: Selected Early Poems. Blue Wind, Berkeley, 1977.

River through Rivertown. Poems. The Figures, Great Barrington, Mass., 1982.

Magpie Rising: Sketches from the Great Plains. Pruett Publishing/ Vintage Books, 1988/1990.

Sworn Before Cranes. Stories. Crown Publishing, 1994.

On Heart River. Poems. Dayo Books, Denver, 1995.

Burnt House to Paw Paw: Appalachian Notes. Hard Press, West Stockbridge, Mass., 1997.

Satin Street. Poems. Moyer Bell Publishers, Wakefield, R.I., 1997.

Chokecherry Places. Johnson Books, Boulder, Colo., 1998.

Grasshopper Falls

Merrill Gilfillan

For Barb
w/ best regards —
Merrill Gilfillan
November 2000

Hanging Loose Press
Brooklyn, New York

Published by Hanging Loose Press, 231 Wyckoff Street, Brooklyn, New York 11217. All Rights Reserved. No part of this book may be reproduced without the publisher's written permission, except for brief quotations in reviews.

Printed in the United States of America
10 9 8 7 6 5 4 3 2 1

Hanging Loose Press thanks the Literature Program of the New York State Council on the Arts for a grant in support of the publication of this book.

Some of these stories first appeared in *Arshile, Hanging Loose* and *Sniper Logic.* Note: The brief speculation about melancholy in the story "Talk Across Water" is based on a passage by philosopher Sheldon Wolin in his essay "Revolutionary Action Today."

Cover photo by author.
Cover design by Pamela Flint

Library of Congress Cataloging-in-Publication Data

Gilfillan, Merrill
        Grasshopper Falls / Merrill Gilfillan.
            p. com
        ISBN 1-882413-69-5 (cloth)—ISBN 1-882413-68-7 (pbk.)
            1. West (U.S.)—Social life and customs—Fiction. 2. Indians
    of North America—West (U.S.)—Fiction. I. Title.
    PS3557.13447 G72 1999
    813'.54—dc21   99-052242

 Produced at The Print Center, Inc. 225 Varick St., New York, NY 10014, a non-profit facility for literary and arts-related publications. (212) 206-8465

Contents

Uncle and Shrike

—with sumac candelabra

They were camped on the Arikaree River, six cars and six tents in a small palm of a place out of the wind. They had been there a few weeks, judging from the camp sprawl and the flat of the grass. They drove old Cadillacs and Continentals showing rust along the running boards—onetime Tory clans from the looks of it. We—my uncle and I—were pitched up on a knoll directly across the river.

My uncle surveyed them with binoculars now and then, our first days there, sized up their little camp, and finally deciphered their license plates. And one morning we cut down through the brushy bottom and crossed the near-dry river to talk. They came from Pennsylvania and had been on the move for a year and a half now. They were jokey, good-tempered people; we could hear them laughing on and off throughout the day and every evening they built two big fires and played canasta or gin rummy on card tables set up tandem between them with greasy brown bags of popcorn on the side.

It was a good place for a spring camp—the cool well water and the river bottom shelter—and it was far enough from the major highways that not everyone on the move showed up, although it wasn't unusual to find a new tent or step-van in camp when I crawled out from our lean-to in the early morning. Most of the passersthrough would stay two or three days, shy and uneasy, visiting with the Pennsylvanians and my uncle, asking about places to summer, or winter, about places with good wood and water and no trouble, worrying about gasoline, asking how to eat chokecherries and what could be done with the hackberries that hung dry on their trees all winter. Then one morning after a prolonged breakfast and the shaking of the blankets they would load up and drive away. But my uncle and I and the Pennsylvanians stayed for a while. We liked it there.

My uncle had me for the summer (that's the way the family put it). He wanted to show me things—things, I know now, that not everyone saw. Things he wanted to see again for himself while he was still able. He met me at the Cheyenne bus station in late May, bought me a hamburger, then drove straight north for an hour and a half with a look of intense concentration on his lean old face. He said little until we made our first official stop at a bridge over a puddle-wide little flow through the eastern Wyoming grasslands. He walked me down through the ditch and over to the right bank of the stream. There was a cattail or two. We stood for a moment gazing down at it, then he turned to me with a wry grin and made the formal introduction: "Here we have the headwaters of the Niobrara River."

And then we began to drive. We cut east into Nebraska, utterly hurryless, stopping often for this thing or that, camping where we felt like it in our tarp lean-to. In the Sandhill country south of the Niobrara we drove out each evening at sunset to any given promontory to sit there in the car with sandwiches and a warm Thermos watching the fireflies come on in the lake valleys below. I had never seen fireflies before—the sandwiches lasted a good long time. The third night out we hit it right: an entire vast oblong valley was pulsing with a collective phosphorescence so dense the black oval of the lake stood out like ink from the flashing lightfield around it. My uncle, after a quarter hour, poured another cup of coffee and told me the story of Benvenuto Cellini and the lizard: How Benvenuto and his father were sitting quietly before the fireplace one night when a beautifully colored lizard darted from the woodpile, so beautiful and so gratuitous that the father reached out and struck Benvenuto across the cheek to ensure that the boy would never lose the moment and its unexpected brilliance.

It was a noble story, I remember thinking; I liked the warm orange hearthglow in it and the sense of esthetic chivalry. When we finished our suppers a few minutes later and were having a last gaze at the flickering valley, my uncle reached over through the dark of the car and gave me a quick, halfhearted cuff on the back of my head.

Life was quiet on the Arikaree, save for the occasional thunder-storm blasting out of the west, when everyone ran to their cars to wait it out. My uncle was a great reader. He carried a duffelbag of old paperbacks in the trunk, as well as a grocery box of particular favorites on the backseat. The first day in camp he had found his offi-cial reading spot under a clump of chokecherry saplings and he moved his chair around it to stay in or out of the sun as the thermals dictated. On cool mornings he took short arthritis-slowed walks along the river, invariably bringing back a specimen or two from the outer world: a feather or an odd stone or an old coyote turd dried unto nothing but silvery mouse hair in a neat peristaltic braid. He arranged them on the folding table in a kaleidoscopic still-life. When he wasn't walking or reading or napping in the shade he often sat silently for great lengths of time staring far off and muttering intently.

There were no boys my age in the camp across the river, but I made friends with a girl named Tina who was somewhere near twelve. We played catch with a rubber ball, and later marbles, a free-form sort of marbles called toss-and-chase, a nearly pointless game that led us far from camp, often out of the river bottom and up the hills until we would look out over the Arikaree prairies and be star-tled to find ourselves there in the midst of all that afternoon light and air and just stand for a moment with our cat's-eyes in our hands. For supper my uncle made macaroni with oleo and chopped salami or sardines, or corn mush with a can of tomatoes stirred in, and we ate and talked a little and watched the night come in.

One morning there was a strange car just upriver from the main camp, wedged into the edge of a thicket as if to hide, with an old green tent by its side. An hour later a man and a woman could be seen shuffling around the site, and then a boy about my size. But they stayed to themselves all day and seemed to avoid even looking in our direction. The following day I wandered up the river toward their place and surprised the boy fiddling around on the muddy bank. He was a ruffled, edgy sort of lad wearing abundant corduroys with the cuffs turned up half a foot above his sneakers. He hurried off into the trees before I reached him.

The family stayed on the Arikaree for five days and never approached our camp, or the Pennsylvanians either. My uncle thought their license plate said Maine. I saw the boy idling privately through the bottoms once or twice. He seemed to carry on a contin-uous conversation with himself, gesturing eloquently or waving one diplomatic explanatory hand like a Gypsy in a phone booth. Some of the younger kids from the Pennsylvania camp said that they had approached him and tried to make acquaintance but he growled at them; that he had a bad tooth he sucked on malevolently and blew the stink at them as he backed away into the bushes.

None of these people had houses anymore. Just the cars and the tents or trailers. Some of them had relatives with homes somewhere, whom they could visit now and then and store excess belongings in a barn or shed and pick up their mail twice a year. But none of them had houses anymore. They moved from camp to camp on a shuttle of need and whimsy. They were used to it by now and most everyone in America was used to them. Winters they hugged the Mexican border and the Florida panhandle, Lake Mead and the Salton Sea. Summers they preferred the hinterland western camps because they were usually far from complications and seldom crowded.

My uncle and I had been on the Arikaree two weeks. The folding table had saucers and bowls full of specimens by then. An ancient key, a magpie cranium and a rock resembling a prime lamb chop and assorted prairie grasses. Early one morning I was drinking my coffee alone at the table when I heard an unaccustomed sound not far off behind a plum thicket: a steady series of small percussions that sounded like a temperamental cap pistol in the still morning. Tap, tap, tap, bang. Tap, tap, bang. I finished my coffee and walked quietly to the thicket and around one edge until I saw an old green Ford Falcon station wagon that had obviously pulled in during the night. It had canvas-wrapped gear and a spare tire lashed on the roof.

With another step I saw an old man sitting Indian fashion on an open sleeping bag in the sun. He was hunched over a flat stone, deeply absorbed in working his way through a roll of caps, striking them one by one with an egg-size cobble. I could smell the old familiar burnt powder hanging in the cool air. Then he sensed me and looked up.

"I haven't done this in a long time."

I stood quietly until he finished the roll, then I told him who I was and where I came from—the other side of the plum patch—and squatted down to watch him from a courteous distance. He took another roll from his shirt pocket and draped the loose end across the stone. He seemed to enjoy the audience. He said he was going to California to see his sister; she still had a house and a yard full of flowers on the outskirts of Sacramento. The man was tall and thin. He had white eyelids, like a magpie, that flashed each time he blinked. But the caps were the main thing at the moment and neither of us said much while he tapped and banged away. When he finished the second roll he stood up and gave one great satisfied clap of his hands and sent me back to my camp with two sugared doughnuts.

Late that afternoon my uncle and I walked over to see him. We chatted for half an hour. This time, maybe it was the time of day, the newcomer seemed distant and memory-sick, but to me he was so far an adult of possible interest. He was still there the next day, and after supper we walked over again and sat with him into sunset eating malted milk balls and drinking coffee.

He was garrulous this time. He told jerking stories of the old days on Lake Erie, stories (there were mallards flying over) of duck and goose hunting camps on the marshes east of Toledo. As a teenager he had worked with the head decoy man at one of the big duck clubs, the indispensable man who raised and trained the live goose decoys, keeping them "just right" between half-wild and half-tame, grooming his small flock to sail forth from their holding pen at just the right moment and swing out over the gray bay to the wild flocks-of-passage and coax them back to the shore, where the gunners were congregated in elaborate underground bunker-blinds, smoking cigars and sipping whiskey until the signal bell rang and they trotted off to their shooting posts and readied for the incoming flock. In the low firelight he conjured handsome images of legendary decoy broods, each bird with a name, ranging day after day in perfectly choreographed maneuvers high above the lake, controlled from afar by a fingertip wizardry in the mind of the trainer.

Then, after rinsing the coffeepot, he sat down and launched another story, his eyelids flashing. A story with different colors this time. A man and his twenty-year-old son were hunting ducks on Lake Erie in November. They were settled in a blind far from shore; they rowed a skiff out to it and tied it under the camouflage. About midday a storm blew in out of nowhere. Before the men could react their skiff was torn loose and gone. They were caught in what was soon a blizzard. The son decided in desperation to wade in to shore before it was utterly hopeless. (The storyteller's voice had dropped to a hoarse curmudgeonly whisper.) So the young man struck off in his hip boots for shore. He made it 50 yards before he foundered, sank to his thighs in the bay muck and couldn't go on. And there was his father watching from the blind, just able to see the boy through the snow, thrashing and shouting as the water rose and the—

My uncle jumped to his feet. "I don't care to hear any more of this story." He pulled me up from the ground, saying goodnight as we walked off into the dark.

Back at our camp he was moody and restless. He perked up our fire and paced at the edge of the light, tossing my rubber ball in one hand.

Finally he stopped and said, "He had his hands all over that story." He was thinking hard as he spoke. "That's not the way it's done. When you tell a story you treat it like you would a person. You don't put your dirty hands all over it just to make someone shiver or run scared."

He was leaning heavily on the table, thinking it through bit by bit. "You look at the world and the people in it and you think about it with words. It goes back and forth between any person and the world, with the words in between. And to get it right, to see it right without being a four-flusher or a fool, you have to slow down, and to do that you have to slow your words down."

He paced a while more, tossing the ball, then came to sit beside me.

"The Arapaho word for blackbird is *hitecouceiiwanahuut*. The word for turtle is *niiceciana baaba*. For chickadee, *ceciitcenihiin*." He made me repeat the chickadee word twice. "These words are long and slow to say so that they will teach a person to be patient in the brain, patient in the talk, so he will have room each time he pronounces them to see and hear how the words fit into the world, how they throw a little net around things and bring them back in to the mind. They teach a person to use them and what they stand for with respect—and to keep their dirty hands off things that don't deserve it! … Dog fennel! I'm going to bed."

He wanted to show me the head of the Smoky Hill River. We packed up on a cool cloudy morning and drove up out of the breaks. The Pennsylvanians were still there. Tina and a few adults waved back at us as we crested the hill.

We drove south on the smallest paved roads we could find— gravel roads ate up the tires—weaving back and forth across the Kansas-Colorado border through the high plain that lay dark and ill at ease under matte cloudlight. By midday we came to a narrow bridge over the river and my uncle pulled off the road and sat for a moment looking off. Then he got out and put a few things in a mesh potato sack and we walked off over a spent fence and upstream along the river for a hundred yards.

The Smoky Hill at this point was little more than a rill, even though it was June. It swung wearily through the grasslands, two, maybe three feet wide, its banks bare save for an occasional runty willow. But my uncle walked right up to it and turned to me and announced ceremoniously, "The headwaters of the Smoky Hill River," and gave me the same sly boyish grin he had used back on the upper Niobrara. Then we sat down in a stand of last year's burnt-out mullein stalks on the north shore and ate Velveeta cheese and tangerines.

We knew there was a camp down on Ladder Creek not far from the town of Modoc, Kansas, and after my uncle napped for half an hour beside the Smoky Hill we drove down there. It was a small flat place with a few box elders and a water pump in the middle of a huge mud puddle where scores of wasps and damselflies came calling. Three cars and a large tent sat at one end of the grounds.

The people in the big tent were on their way to a small chapel somewhere in Nevada to see an icon of Christ that wept real tears each day at sunset accompanied by a grievous band of pigeons on the eaves outside. The camp was a dull one except for the several riverbends and their thinning trees, but we stayed for a time. My uncle was in the midst of a fat book and wanted to get through it before we moved along. And he had spotted a ranch pond just up the road with an inviting "No Fishing, Don't Ask" sign tacked to one of its trees. Each evening at dusk we walked over there and he slipped through the fence and threw in trotlines baited with bacon rind. In the morning I would hear him returning before I was up from bed, carrying a stringer of nice bullheads, which he tethered in a Ladder Creek pool until suppertime, when he skinned them with pliers and rolled them in cornmeal and fried them and everyone in camp stopped and sniffed the air. One day he caught a snapping turtle, which he traded to an Alabama family for grapefruits and a jar of blackstrap molasses.

I explored the little river in both directions, whiling away the warmer and warmer days, climbing trees and reading *Robin Hood*. One morning I discovered a newcomer lying in the sun beside a muddy pool downstream from camp. She was a stout white-skinned woman with cropped tow hair. She rolled over when she heard me step through the brush and put one hand over her eyes to look.

Finally she said, "If you'd've been here ten minutes earlier you'd've caught me buck naked." She had a deadpan, farmer sort of voice.

It was a startling image, I knew that instantly, and I knew I would walk many miles out of the way to avoid seeing this person buck naked. She was stocky, strong, and very pale, a negative out-from-under-the-stone pale. She wore denim clothes and had tiny chewed nails on short-digited hands, pale blue eyes reminiscent of a too-hot sky. She was most certainly tough as dirt and unshakable—beyond doubt an adult of possible interest.

She was a dogcatcher from a rural county in Missouri. She had been to Oklahoma for a funeral and was lazing here on Ladder Creek for a while before the final run home. This was the first vacation she had taken in ten years, she said, not counting the opening day of trapping season, which she took off annually to get her muskrat traps deployed. She was driving her dogcatcher truck, she told me, with seven homeless dogs in the back because she was unable to find anyone trustworthy back home to feed them for a week.

She was lying on one side, propped on her elbow on a beach towel. She exuded through her faint eyes and blank-white skin a primitive pastoral aplomb that almost attained suavity. Her center of gravity was low and calm, with a fleck of cunning that could have survived, even thrived, at a fashionable cocktail party. As I said good-bye and turned to go she cleared her throat and repeated her opening sentence verbatim in the exact pitch and tone. "If you'd've been here ten minutes earlier you'd've caught me buck naked." That night as the moon came up—we were eating bullheads and cottage cheese with grape jelly on it; my uncle was saying, "Two dollars for cottage cheese! Hell's fire! When I was a boy we gave it to the chickens"—we heard her truckload of dogs crooning from across the river.

I visited her camp the next forenoon and every morning thereafter. Her name was Trixie. She always wore the same denim pants and jacket over a gray workshirt. Looking back on it, I suppose she was thirty-five or forty years old. One day I found her loafing in the shade of her truck, cleaning her nails with a jack knife, leaning against two huge sacks of dog food. She said she was about to run her dogs, if I cared to see it, and got up to unbar the door of the cage.

The seven mutts poured out from the truck and swarmed around her, a hodgepodge of reds and browns and yellows. She picked up a thin bamboo cane, the kind you might win at a county fair game, and waved it over the animals once and they were instantly quieted. "They know better," she said. "I do this twice a day, rain or shine." Then she sent them off with a guttural "git" and we watched them course in remarkable coordination around the wide flats north of the river. If they moved too far away she called and waved the cane and the pack responded. They reminded me (or maybe they simply remind me now) of the trained goose flocks working their remote-controlled chore-life over Lake Erie. The dogs hullied right or left, fore and aft, as she commanded.

I returned next day to watch them again. Trixie told me on the side how to catch a mink and blow eggs and take a live skunk from a trap. That last afternoon I saw them run, when the dogs were back in their cage and the sun was just in the treetops, Trixie sat down and looked at me a long time with her flat blue eyes and asked how old I was. Then she began to talk in a low country-store kind of voice, the lilting provincial voice that charms and fascinates with its cardinal sureness and its lexical world of absolute jerkwater certainty. She began tossing out blunt, seemingly random tidbits of confidential lore from her hometown in Missouri. She knew a farm boy about my age who was getting sexy with a milking machine and got stuck in it. She looked at me matter-of-factly for a sly moment to see how that registered. She knew a man who could squeeze milk from his own nipples. She knew of a man, a highway patrolman, who had three balls. The stories got fancier and fancier, but her coded vocabulary was so coy and so far beyond mine—she was bandying rapid-fire about so-and-so's cooter, japus, or mojo—that I was never exactly sure I was getting the right picture. She went on and on, pausing long sacerdotal seconds between each folkloric tableau, all in a hypnotic monotone so flat she might have been calling a bingo game—until my uncle whistled me over for dinner.

She left early the following morning. She would be home in time to run her dogs before dark. Like all of the people that summer she had loomed and faded suddenly, but she left an abrupt imprint all her own. I realized much later that she was a scion of peasantry held over from the age of the Breughels. I would no more have cared to meet her again than I would have cared to see her buck naked in the first place. But for several pubescent years whenever I heard mention of Missouri I thought of her briefly, of her cartoon village and the sideshow menagerie of people in a state of constant, furtive semi-arousal, with something like a toy train whistle sounding far off behind.

Then my uncle finished the long book he was reading and we packed up. We drove half a day south into the Gila monster country, bought groceries, and then curled easterly and found an almost empty camp on Pawnee Creek not too far from the town of Jetmore. We set up our lean-to in the lee of a thicket, as always, and had several quiet days to ourselves.

My uncle always insisted on waiting a short time between books, so he sat a lot along Pawnee Creek, gazing off at the skyline or an old cottonwood for hours. He would come to find me sometimes where I was playing alone or annoying an anthill. He would squat for a while watching, reach out and stroke my head one time, then get up and walk nervously away, slapping his thighs in rhythm to some inner Dixieland type of tune.

I was ill at ease and even frightened when he sat so long gazing, sailing out so far. It left me too much alone. A few years earlier I had visited him at a time when he still had a small house. It was May and he was making his beloved garden in the same old backyard spot, and I helped a little. Only that year I gradually realized he had lost control of it. He measured out and hoed his wobbly furrows and then forgot to plant the seed; or planted one row properly, then proceeded to cover the rest of the unplanted furrows in the section, tamping them carefully with the back of his hoe. At the end of the week no one had any idea what, if anything at all, might come up where.

If I went to join him in his reverie, as I often did on Pawnee Creek out of fear and loneliness, if I went slowly to him and sat on the earth near his folding chair, he would gradually come back home, stir a bit, drum his fingers on his knees, and mutter a sentence or two about a red-haired girl from Tennessee he had dated years ago: She was musical, a singer; she had "elf ears." One afternoon he came back detailing a favorite incident from the family past, the fact that his mother had stood before Geronimo as he made his mark on scraps of paper and sold them to tourists at the 1904 St. Louis World Fair. And then he would come all the way back and stand up and clap his hands three or four times and say, "What I wouldn't give for a bowl of Michigan blueberries and an Indiana musk melon!"

There was no bullhead pond at Pawnee Creek so we were back to macaroni and variable rice stews. When the time was right my uncle pulled a Thomas Wolfe novel from the duffel and started on it for what he said was the fourth time. He called me over now and then and read me a long sinewy sentence or a favorite passage as he sat within a small dome of lantern light.

Then we started east, moving a little faster than usual. We were headed for the Kaw River, a camp just west of Topeka. We drove short, easy back road days once we left Pawnee Creek, but we camped at each place for just a night. My uncle wanted to be at the Kaw before the summer got too far along. We put up at the Cheyenne Bottoms near the Arkansas River, at a damp camp on the Little Arkansas east of Hutchison, and then at Cottonwood Creek out from Emporia. I might be forgetting one. We always paused for a nice long lunch by some stream or other and then a nap for my uncle, and stopped religiously to back up and look at dead snakes on the road, but we kept moving, in our way, toward the Kaw in order to get there before the summer boiled over: He wanted me to hear the eastern bird songs.

We drove into the Kaw River camp on the Fourth of July. It was a big camp, almost like a town. It went for a good ways along the river. There were all kinds of tents and huts and trailers, with makeshift alleys threading through. There were more trees on the Kaw than anywhere else we had been and everyone had their shade to rest in.

We took a walk through camp after we were set up and stowed. There were cars from all over the country. Some families were hawking things like tires or tarps or parched corn. None of these people had homes anymore. They were strikingly neither happy nor sad. That evening just at dark about half the camp climbed the hills south of the river and sat silently watching the tiny fireworks on the horizon going up out of Topeka and some of the small towns to the north.

There were fish in the Kaw and at suppertime the whole camp smelled of them frying. One family was selling lemons. Three consecutive mornings my uncle roused me before daybreak, handed me a quick breakfast, and led me by the elbow to a sizable uninhabited grove downriver. We stood leaning against a cottonwood and waited quietly as the first light came. Then the birds in the river trees began to sing. My uncle nudged me in case I'd forgotten why we were there. First one tree, then another, and another, until the entire congregation was in full voice around us.

"These are birds you'll never hear in the West," he whispered. "Listen to them while you can."

We stood there for half an hour each of the three mornings and then walked back to camp. My uncle fished a little in the Kaw and I explored the neighborhood. There were plenty of boys to throw the ball with. Sometimes we saw cars of people—from Topeka, probably—drive up onto the hills above camp and sit there a while looking down at us all. It was hot and dusty; then it rained. There was a fight one evening after dark, and one day they brought in three teenagers knotted up sick in the back of a pickup. They had eaten jimson weed and were in bad shape. The parents jumped in the back of the truck and they rushed off to find a hospital.

But my uncle wasn't feeling very good. He had lots of spells that week. He would wander off suddenly to the riverbank and sit there looking, in that way that left me far behind. I tried to keep him in as close as I could with my usual tactics, easing over to sit beside him, or asking a trivial question, or, finally, clowning in front of him, walking elaborately backwards to and fro across his field of vision.

And he recited more of the odd wind-borne little stories as they came to him. One about his high school girlfriend, a country girl he hadn't seen since 1927 until he attended a class reunion fifty years later, and was standing talking with old friends when the door opened and there she was—"Lissy"—with her husband and a face full of wrinkles and stoved-up hands. She recognized my uncle and turned and ran from the building and never returned.

And one he told half proudly about a sad farm widow with children he had talked out of suicide during dark days of the Depression when he was employed as a relief worker, his first job. I carved him a backscratcher from a willow branch.

But I could see he was traveling farther and farther away. He slept a lot there by the Kaw, as if that place, the farthest extent and turn-around point of our summer, was also a sort of apogee for his inner orbiting. I watched him as he napped on a bedspread under a tree. Now and then he would click like an electric oven going on and off. I thought hesitantly about his life, of his many wanderings and manifold interests. Well-schooled, he had finally taken a job with a hatchery, driving truckloads of new chicks here and there about the prairie states. Driving, because he loved elemental motion; the prairie states, he told me, because he could read a good bit at the wheel.

I pondered as I watched him in deep ocean sleep just what exactly becomes of all the learnings, the lifetime of lore and burnished, relished detail. What would happen one day to all his brief jokes and off-color puns and spirited wit and simple love of earthly things. What would become of "Dog fennel!", "Finer than frog hair," and "Oh what a bag Dad had"? It was as if the whole affectional inner life, delicate as an ear, was slowly leaking while he slept and disappearing, slipping into the Kaw, then the Missouri, the Mississippi, and off. And I was afraid for us both.

But other days he would be right back in the world, determined to figure its particulars. He drove me over toward Topeka one morning. A man had told him about a great stormfall of trees in the valley, aftermath of a blaster blow last spring. Many of the downed trees were sycamores, the man said. That excited my uncle; he wanted me to see the great white boles. We spent half a morning moving through the wreckage of the storm. It was odd to walk familiarly among the bright upper branches of the large trees, admiring the intimate dapple of their sky-limbs at rest. My uncle was quick to point out that the sycamores were all fallen in a uniform direction, aligned almost magnetically amid the drab jumble of the non-sycamore mess, and I could sense his silent groping to explain.

Shortly thereafter we left the big-city camp and started back west. We camped a rainy night at a pull-off somewhere near Hollis, Kansas, and the following day found a pretty camp on a curve of the Republican River. There was a threesome of old Airstream trailers set up there with lots of people in them. They had their old folks gathered in a small snow fence pen, sitting on folding chairs and pitting chokecherries and dropping them into a kettle.

My uncle was bound to finish the book he was reading before we parted, so we stayed on the Republican for a week. Within two days there was a pile of buffalo gourds stacked like cannonballs on the table beside a snakeskin and a giant black beetle. It was chicory season, the "blue time," and we took short drives in the late afternoons to see the pools and swales of the off-blue blossoms with the lowering sun on them. And there were bowls of sugared wild black currants after supper.

When the John Ruskin was finished and returned to the duffel we headed out for our final camp. My uncle decided it would be fitting to go back to the Arikaree River for a couple of days. We drove up the Beaver River for a long way and then cut west to our old camp. We set up in exactly the same spot we had occupied in June. The Pennsylvanians were gone, the girl with the bag of cat's-eyes was gone; grass was growing back where they had worn it down. There was a family camped across the way. Californians. They were busy all day hanging and tending white cloth sacks in the lower box elder branches. They were trying to make some sort of cheese.

My uncle and I just rested, paused in a formal tacitly agreed-upon way. We watched the magpies ride the wind down a long steep hill over and over, flying slowly back up to the top to do it again, like sledders with their sleds, then sailing effortlessly down in scalloping, rollicking swoops. In another day or two he would take me to Cheyenne and put me on a bus for Reno and he would drive back to his bachelor hotel in Ogallala where he was the only non-cowboy in the bunch. But he got along fine. He slept on a bedroll on his fire escape at least six months of the year. His room, I knew, was stacked with books belt-high all around the walls.

We had driven a nice big watermelon of a loop on that trip and we were both pleased with it. We didn't discuss it much, the trip or its being almost over, but my uncle did give me a sheet of paper with a list of his ancestors' burial places—sleepy, saggy-fenced rural grave-yards across Indiana and Ohio and down into western Virginia—and requested that if I ever in my life got that way I might drop a peony here or there on his behalf.

Our last morning in camp, after we loaded up, my uncle took a slow stiff-legged walk up into the Arikaree hills. I sat on the fender of the car and quietly moped. He was gone a good while and I was beginning to feel frightened underneath the mope. Then I heard him holler and saw him far up on the hill, hollering and waving for me to come up.

I knew he must have found something good. I hurried up the dry slope and down through a gully head and over to where he was standing grinning beside a small thorn tree. Hung about the branches were an assortment of small creature carcasses—mice, shrews, and a small bird or two impaled carefully on the thorns.

"A shrike tree," he said, beaming. "I haven't seen one in years."

It looked like a sort of bedeviled Neanderthal Christmas tree. My uncle leaned in from all sides and stood on tiptoe to examine the specimens. He pointed at a broken chickadee on one of the limbs, looked at me, and enunciated slowly: *ceciitcenihiin.* That was the very climactic thing he had been searching for the past few days, the perfect casual but cabalistic closing of the summer's circle.

We went over every carcass on that shrike tree, studying them, lift-ing them carefully with a sharp pencil, on that hot dry hill above the Arikaree, and by the time we were finished we had both shaken our mopes and lost our silly fear for the world and we drove away toward Wyoming.

Tailwind

The men left the car along the dirt road and walked down a pine-choked draw to the cliff, and there was the wide Tongue River valley off below them and a dozen sudden meadowlark songs washing up through the May air. The beautiful old river oxbowed at her ease through sweet hay meadows and sagebrush flats. Her big cottonwood stands were ashimmer with half-grown leafage wild with the sun and the low willows cast a soft red haze to the bottomland. On both edges of the mile-broad valley rose the bluffs with their own deep earth-red glimmering through the black pines.

The white man knew the way and went first down the trail and the black man followed. They talked in the hushed, ready tones of fishermen approaching water. Soon they were in the valley and rigging their gear and eyeing the strong spring flow of the Tongue.

"We can find walleyes down in here. They come up from the big dam. And there are always lots of crappies to get into." The white man was older. He had lived in the area for twenty-five years and was showing the black man where to fish. They worked at the national forest ranger station down the road. They moved to the riverbank and walked along it, watching the water work. "I haven't seen a game warden in here in ten years," the white man whispered. "They say the last time one came around he found a bunch of Indian boys with a mess of illegal fish and a pile of young turkeys. They stripped him down and ran an eight-inch perch up his arse and left him there. He had to have surgery to get the damned thing out."

They began casting into a large hole at a river bend where song sparrows skulked in the willows and jumped to the bushtops to sing. The men warmed to the fishing and grew silent, passing each other leapfrog fashion as one of them moved ahead to reach a new hole upstream.

The white man called the black man over to show him a murky slow-water pool where a school of carp were milling. "We don't want to get into those things," the older man said as they moved on. "I'll tell you though, they aren't bad eating if you treat them right. I was stationed in England during the war and I ate a lot of carp over there. I had a girlfriend near the base and her father was a fisherman. He'd bring home carp and be just as proud as if they were trout. They look at them different over there—gussy them up and roast them like a chicken."

He pointed with his rod to a nice pool and motioned the other man in toward it. He moved off a few yards and stopped to bait his hook. He wanted to talk a little more now.

He cast a minnow-jig and told the black man about the English months, good in spite of the war; about the girl, and his voice had a lower pitch to it.

He had wanted that girl more than anything, had chased her hard. Had wanted that whole life, he supposed now. The whole English bit had hit him pretty hard, a boy from Montana.

But it wasn't just that. It was the girl. He was crazy after her, but he couldn't pull it off.

"Just couldn't get it into high gear," he said in the husky fishing whisper. "Marge has been a wonderful wife to me. But that girl was the one I wanted."

He reeled in a nice crappie and knelt to put it on the stringer. He was off into it now and enjoying it: He began to mimic a British accent as he chatted and the black man smiled at the sea change.

"I say, that's the ticket," the old man said, climbing up the bank.

They fished along steadily, keeping the larger crappies and an occasional walleye. They stopped and walked out onto a broad sage flat where the old man smoked a pipe and looked up at the two-tone bluffs, red on the upper half and white below, and the darker hill-mountains beyond. Then they went back to the fishing.

When they rounded a bend they saw a blue tent on the bank fifty yards ahead and an Indian boy sitting on the ground beside it. The white man waved and after a moment of consideration said, "That's

Tommy, I think. What's he up to, I wonder."

Soon they reached the spot and the white man talked to the Cheyenne fellow while he fished. The boy sat by the tent listening to Merle Haggard on a tape player. His camp was tucked neatly between a dense willow brake and the river, in the shade of a large cottonwood.

"You don't mind if I fish in your front yard do you, Tommy?" the white man said. The boy smiled and said no.

"You better get them while you can," the boy said. "Before the strip mines poison them all off."

"We won't let that happen, now will we, old chap," the man said as he flipped his jig across the stream. He was still flashing a British facet in his sentences whether he knew it or not. It had become the tenor of the morning.

The white man introduced the black man to Tommy. The boy shook hands with the man and grinned: "Red, white, and black—the American flag." He showed the two men a stringer staked to the bank; three nice catfish swayed on it.

"That's what I've been living on the last couple of days."

The black man nodded at the boy and moved on to fish. Through the willows he could hear Tommy and the old man's chat and friendly sparring: the soft northern clip of the boy and then the preposterous would-be British patter of the man, so incongruous it made the black man laugh aloud and shake his head as he fished. The last thing he heard was the boy: "Everyone knows the white man is possessed by the devil."

Ten minutes upstream the old man caught up with him, moving to his side and startling him at a large hole bellying under a tawny earthen cliff.

"This is a good hole, Roger. There's always walleye in here." They stood on a sandbar baiting up.

"That Tommy is a good sort. One of his brothers was a bit of a rotter, though. Tommy worked for me one summer clearing fire roads. He lives up in Billings.

"But a bit of a Lothario, I dare say. Right now he's laying low—that's why the campout. Hiding from a Cree girl who's got the goods on him. He might eat a hell of a lot of catfish before that's all over."

There was a shift in the sunny air, a tack, and the brief crystalline chill of endless need and pull, of all the warm-blooded tonnage and its scattered muddy entrepôts. The white man had rigged his jig and moved carefully toward the upper end of the pool.

"Quite right," he whispered in a pencil-mustached little voice. "Off we go."

Grasshopper Falls

There was a dog of note living along one stretch of the Paint Creek highway. You would see her, a calico half-terrier, every summer day working the backwater reservation road. She survived entirely on her own, subsisting on grasshoppers and other insects struck down by passing traffic. Of course she had to compete with the neighborhood birds for the bounty; she learned to use them to locate prey the way fishing boats key on swarms of gulls at sea. Sunday mornings she traveled a mile down the road to a country church and gleaned the grasshoppers from the gathered cars' grilles. But she was otherwise along the upper stretch, combing along the berm with her nose to the ground or sitting on her thin hips beyond the ditch waiting alertly for cars.

The family in the new house not far above the terrier's range had just discovered an old man near starvation in a shack far back in the canyoned hills. The family had been back there in their pickup truck—it was rough country getting in and out—gathering berries the day before. They all knew the small once-blue shack at the edge of a stream, they passed it every year on their berry run. But none of them knew the old man sitting almost in a stupor on the ground outside, leaning against the wall.

The man seemed too weak to even speak. He was dark and shrunken, his long thinning white hair pushed back over large ears. He looked solemnly from one face to the other of the family, sat flat and listless against the shack and finally closed his eyes. The pump in the yard worked. Inside the door the mother of the family found a coffee can of water and a washbasin holding a handful of berries. There was a wooden crate turned upside down with a package of limp saltines and a box of bluetip matches on it and a hairy cow-licked blanket spread on the floor.

The family leaned over the old man and talked to him slowly, asked if he were sick, if anyone else lived in the shack, would he like to come down with the family and find someone to help him out. He shook his head at each question and closed his eyes. Finally the mother left a ham sandwich and a Pepsi and three cigarettes on the ground beside him and told him they would be back with food as soon as possible.

And now today they were all trying to find out who the old man was. They asked everyone who lived along the Paint Creek highway; everyone knew the shack, but had never heard of anyone living up there for twenty years now. The mother called people around the district, asking for advice, asking if anyone had heard about an old man all by himself up in the canyon hills.

They sent Hamilton and another boy back this morning in the pickup. They carried the old man a bucket of soup and a loaf of bread and a box of donuts and a muskmelon and a bag of smoking tobacco. They found him sitting on the floor just inside the shack. He looked at the soup a long time and finally began to sip it with a large arthritic spoon. Hamilton and the other boy sat with him a half hour and then drove down the hill.

People had heard about the old man by now and began to stop by the family's house to learn the details. There was a good crowd there when Hamilton got back, men and women standing around the living room drinking coffee. One of them was inquiring about the old man's appearance. The father described him: a little bit of a man, kind of stoop-shouldered, long white hair going bald on the top. The people listened carefully. One old man seated on the couch (he might have fit the description himself) coughed and asked, "Does he have all of his fingers on both hands?"

The father of the family said he thought so, and turned to Hamilton as he entered the room. "Did you see if the old man has got all his fingers?"

The boy said, "Yeah, he's got them all."

The man on the couch nodded slowly and settled back in his seat. "If he won't say anything, tomorrow we can call the Elderly Council and report it to them. Maybe they know if anyone is missing."

"From the look of it he's been up there a long time," the mother said. "I bet he's been there all summer." She was making a fresh pot of coffee. "I wish Edna was here. I bet she would know who he is. She knows everyone west of the Missouri River."

"We should let Edna know about it. She might know the man right away."

So they asked Hamilton if he would ride over to see Edna and her family on English Creek and tell them about the man and what he looked like.

"Take the three-wheeler," his father said.

It was a long ride cross-country to Edna's place, up and down hills and across two creeks, so Hamilton sat and ate a lunch before he started up the three-wheel cycle and left the yard.

The boy was a quiet, ponderous fifteen. He was just showing signs of an early plumpness and wore large dark-framed glasses strapped to his head with elastic. He loved solitary errands more than anything. He loved their blend of solitude and prescribed destination because he tended toward the contemplative end of the constitutional spectrum and often was faintly alarmed to find himself sitting stolidly for long periods under a tree or beside a river, wondering about things. He wondered about water and ice. About the unbending purple of the harebells. About the muscle of souls and the gristle of opinion perpetually halving. He wondered about the flight of birds, wondered if the big cottonwood groves by the rivers filtered the air of the spiritual acridity of human malfeasance the way they took the carbon dioxide from their lungs, the way vultures cleaned the roads. He wondered why some days he was sad as a Jain. This pensiveness would make him proud later in his life; he would cultivate it as a proper metaphysician, a thinking man, but at age fifteen it sometimes annoyed him, like the bulge of superfluous belly above his belt. But it was always there, a quiet background music of ponder almost like a shadow, and his favorite time of day was still sundown, when the colors faded and the lavenders took over and softened the brittle borders between things. And lately he had found a comfortable, sensible way of wondering. An experienced thinking man in the vicinity, learned and bent almost double, had explained to him that the philosophical life was like the workings of the woodpeckers, their resolute daily searching and prying among the trees for worthwhile things. The man had picked up a twig and tapped with it against a tree trunk, imitating the unobtrusive staccato of a woodpecker at large. He told Hamilton to do the same when he felt like thinking about things; it was a good way to warm up for a mull.

He drove up the dirt road climbing behind his family's house and over the pine-clad ridge, slowing as he dropped down the other side and the road dwindled. A small cloud of white dust followed him. It was a bright August day and everything he saw appeared clean and well-intentioned. He began humming and thinking about the sacred, the *wakan*. He saw that the sunflowers in their swales were *wakan* by virtue of their golden gregariousness and strong necks, and that the flocks of black-and-white buntings flushing up beside the road were *wakan* by the grace of their social two-toned unanimity pretty as piano keys.

He forded the creek at the bottom of the long hill. People called it Grasshopper Creek. There were two mallards there in a pool below a little riffle-falls—*wakan* because they knew how to dress fancy and live invisibly at the same time. Then he was on a narrow road climbing gradually through grassland and scattered pines, a faint dirt road with sweet young sage and white mallow vine trailing along the fenceless edges—and the kingbirds hawking above him were *wakan* simply because they partook of such a day and place, grew from it and larked through it making a cantankerous and indispensable noise.

Within this thought-world of hills and streams, the boy was also thinking of the old man they had found. A man without a name, or with a name that nobody knew. Hamilton had watched him closely for the half hour while he ate the soup that morning, and now the boy found himself remembering something a young man—another thinking man he saw now and again at sweat lodges—had told him several months ago. Of a sudden the man had turned to Hamilton in the last of the sunset as the fire was roaring and popping and said quietly, "No one wants to be born. We're all like those people starving over in Somalia. No one asks people if they want to be born. We just wake up and find ourselves here."

The boy arrived at the second creek—English Creek—and crossed it at a gravelly shallow. He met a man walking along carrying a dead hawk in one hand. Hamilton stopped and the man held the bird up by both wings to show it off like a butterfly, speckled red and gold and black across the shoulders, *wakan* because the sun was on it.

Another mile down the creek Hamilton saw the house where Edna and her family lived. It was a square old stucco under steeply pitched roofs with a good many shingles blown off. Hamilton shut off his cycle and walked to the front door. A crewcut man was working on a car engine near the porch. Inside, Edna and her husband were sitting on a soft couch talking with two boys and a handsome young woman. Edna brought him a cup of coffee.

After a few minutes Hamilton shifted his feet and let go of his message. "You know, we found an old man yesterday, way back in the hills. We were getting berries, and found him sitting by that old blue cabin back there. He didn't have hardly anything to eat. He doesn't say anything to anybody. No one knows who he is."

The old people had stopped everything to watch the boy.

"We took him back some food and left it with him. He ate some soup and smoked some cigarettes. My mother wants to find out where he came from so she can tell someone. He doesn't say a word."

Edna's husband finally asked, "He hasn't got any social security card or nothing in his pockets?"

Then, a moment later, Edna: "How old is the man? What does he look like?"

"He's old," Hamilton said. "He's little and stooped over, with white hair. He wears a red and black flannel shirt."

Edna: "Is that the old cabin on Sweetgrass divide? Along the big breaks?"

"Yes."

"He didn't say nothing? Not even in Indian?"

"He never said a word."

Edna thought for a minute. "Is he a dark-skinned man?"

"Pretty dark."

The two teenaged boys and the girl had gone back to whispering softly among themselves.

"Has he got all his fingers on his hands?"

Hamilton looked up at the old woman. "Yeah, he's got all of them. I saw him rolling cigarettes."

Edna was considering, with lips pursed. "Maybe he used to live back there a long time ago.... Maybe someone didn't want him and took him back there and left him."

After a while she turned to her husband and said, "Maybe we better go over there. We better go and have a look at the man. Maybe we can figure out who he is." The husband agreed and Edna went off to pack up some food for the stranger.

Hamilton wandered out to the porch where the young people had moved. The girl was home from college for the summer. She had long hair in a ponytail that hung below her hips. She was smoking and talking to the boys.

"We should change all the names of places back to the names our people called them. These whiteman names don't mean anything."

She looked over at Hamilton and smiled. She wore long dangle earrings from Oklahoma that stretched her earlobes a little with their weight.

"They named everything the same—Mud Creek or Dry Creek or Castle Rock. They don't know what land is."

She told them how Indians in Canada had changed the spelling of their tribes' names to make them Indian words, not white words. "And the Omahas changed their name to U-ma-ga-hagh. It's more of an Indian word."

The boys nodded and smoked. Hamilton asked her, "How do you change the names of everything when they already have names?"

"You have to make a new map. The Chinese people and the Russians are always changing their names around, to make the words look more like people say them, not like somebody else came in and said them. They change the maps. First it was Peiping, then Peking, and then Beijing. They have people working on that all the time."

Edna and her husband came out with a bag of things. The young people decided they would ride over to Paint Creek with them, and a minute later the man working on the engine decided he would too. Hamilton said he would rest a short while before riding back over the hills.

"Sure, go ahead," Edna's husband said. "In the house or out here, anywhere you want." They all got in the car and drove away.

The boy stood with his hands in his pockets and watched the car ease out the lane toward the valley road. His errand was completed and he was alone again. He looked around, then began to stroll the yard and off among the outbuildings, through the pigweed and past the car with its engine hanging from a gantry. There was a mean-looking hen with a brood of chicks that surely never asked to be hatched—they tore through the world omnivorous and slashing.

Hamilton wondered who the man with missing fingers might be. But he was tired of all the questions and the wondering. Edna could take over for a while; she was a good thinking woman. She would figure out who the man in the shack was and that would be taken care of. For today, Hamilton was tired of it. He would just as soon have a set of purple summer sucker-kisses running down his neck like most of his friends that year.

He would take a little rest. He walked over to the corral and leaned on the fence looking at the horses. As always, standing alone near horses made him think of his great-grandfather. Henry Feather had been a famous bronc hand known all over South Dakota. Hamilton had heard all the stories about him many times. Henry was the ace horsebreaker for a big outfit around here and down into Nebraska. Early this century they sold herds to the Mexican government, and during World War I they had a big contract to furnish cavalry and artillery horses to the French and Italian armies. They sent a lot of horses over there.

The boy walked over and stretched out on the ground under a little tree. He could still smell the corrals. His great-grandfather once rode twenty broncs in a single day. Stories had it that Henry always wanted to know where each of the bronc lots he worked with was headed for; winked and said he taught the horses a little different for each country. Hamilton drowsed. He had a plan of his own: he would think and study and acquire knowledge until he was thirty-five or forty; then he would quit, take it easy, maybe go to live in California for a while. He didn't know if an old man without a name was all that different from one with. But he knew exactly where Henry Feather was buried. He was buried down the road in the hamlet of Lowe, in a patchy-grass and sagebrush cemetery off behind the Catholic church. His brown and gray horses were scattered, far from the meadowlarks, in little pieces all over France.

Men In Shadow

I. Yank-ton-ai

Not far from the Cannonball River, not far from where it disappears into the shackled Missouri, full summer in place. The bright sky, the drumming perpendicular heat, the dust-heavy sunflowers along every road and byway, the heedless grasshoppers, cardboard beer cases smashed in the ditches—have driven the old men, three of them here, into the cool thick shade of a haystack, a tall trefoil of three huge round bales now forgotten as though misplaced and never found, slowly melting toward one shapeless pre-industrial toadstool mass.

The men were at ease on their haunches, leaning against the stack. They had taken off their straw summer Stetsons and set them, each, on the dry ground just off their right knees. It was first-class shade. They could see the small highway not far off, the occasional cars slowing a familiar iota for the old stop sign, and a blanched peach-colored house long empty on a distant treeless knoll. Nearer at hand in the sunflowers and tall grass stood an unknown and unowned mortar-and-wattle hive of a thing, a cracked mud-colored wasp-like oven or kiln, also melting, belt-high under a spindly summer-fey elm.

When a young boy with a popsicle idled up on his bicycle, instinctively edged in under the shade for a moment muttering a little approximate tune to himself, the one old man began to talk. He talked to the other men but thought of the boy while he did.

"I was walking across from Shields the other night. Coming home from my brother's. It was dark already, there wasn't much of a moon. I got to the creek there at the log bridge and stopped for a smoke. I sat down on an old tree stump right there and smoked. Pretty soon I looked across the other way and there was someone over there— I couldn't see anything but their cigarette light up when they smoked on it. I said something out loud. Nobody answered. Just the cigarette burning in the dark with somebody smoking it. So I sat there and finished my smoke, then got up and walked to the bridge. I passed right by that person—from here to that sunflower. I looked as hard as I could but there wasn't anybody there—just that cigarette. It was still there, going on and off like a firefly when I looked back across the bridge."

The other men said nothing. It was six hours till dark. The boy's mouth was coronaed popsicle red all the way around when he pushed off silently, as gradually as he had arrived, and pedaled in an unhurried reflective weave away into the bright sun.

*****

The man on the right, if you stood and faced them, the man on the north, was Eldon Hat. He sat beside his Stetson in the shade. Two days earlier he had received a visitor from Atlanta, Georgia, and it was still with him in a lingersome way, like smoke in your hair or gasoline on your hands.

Donald Hanks had flown from Atlanta to Minneapolis to Bismarck, North Dakota, with the sole purpose of finding Eldon Hat. They had been in the Second War together, shoulder to shoulder through some nasty business, and hadn't seen each other since. Donald wasn't sure even where Eldon was living, if he were living, but he came to North Dakota to find out.

He rented a car at the Bismarck airport and drove south along the Missouri. He glanced at its gulls, then stopped at the store by the Cannonball turnoff to inquire if Eldon Hat was still around. They sent him up the little road along the Cannonball River. When he got to the half-hamlet of Shields he stopped a woman on the road and asked again. She gave him high-pitched directions abstract as ice, but he recognized the house immediately when he got there.

Eldon Hat was resting in his kitchen. He saw the two horses in the yard look up and off toward the road together and his blind deaf dog get up to circle slowly in place and he knew someone was coming to see him.

He recognized Donald Hanks by his huge body and oversized totem-pole grin. He was glad to see him. They shook hands for a long time, then went to sit on two straight chairs in the shade of the sky-blue house. "My wife is at work." They were old men who knew it, one slight and slow, the other large and full of awkward sprawl; his chair braced and groaned. They had exchanged one friendly pair of letters in the spring of 1951, and were about to talk for two hours.

"I'm seventy two come September," Donald was saying. He had a handkerchief in his hand to catch the runnels from his brow. "Forty-four of them went to Waco Scaffolding. Atlanta branch."

Eldon figured for a moment. "That makes you fourteen months older than I am."

"September 9, 1916."

"The third of November, 1917. I've lived here all my life."

"You remember Dave Finney."

"Sure I do." Out of Frankfurt, Kentucky. Lanky, long oatmeal-textured face. A good man, called everyone "Buddy." Professed to love whiskey. Constantly cracking his knuckles. Prayed on his knees every night. He died in a factory explosion in 1975.

"You remember Aaspaugh?" Harry Aaspaugh. "Goosey." Dover, Delaware. Quiet. Always talking quietly about the Bay. Bluefish. Crabs. Gigging frogs from a canvas canoe. Then the big fry, all you could hold. Beer and a half-peck of lemons. The flattest feet they ever let in the army. Left tracks in the shower room big as a grizzly. Laughed at the drop of a hat. But goosey—jumped three feet if you touched him anywhere between the belt and the kneecaps. Worked for Proctor and Gamble. Died of heart, 1980.

And Eddie—Eddie Bainge, with the Barlow knife and the black hair all over his body. He never came home. Buried outside St. Lo— or was it St. Crieuc de Ton?

"You remember Carl Jones." Wichita County, Texas. Smoked Lucky Strikes (green war pack) like candy. "Bones" Jones. A high-cheek-boned lonely distractedness, an innate *noblesse oblige* that kept him leaning. Loved every woman he ever met. Could eat enough for three men. A little older than the rest. He went back to Texas. He died in 1969. Used to sing "I dream of Jeannie with the light brown hair" all day long.

"I thought that was Ebersprecher."

34

And J.T. Murray. He's still alive. Still in Oakland, California. He never misses a Christmas card. "Hurry" Murray. A great poker player, but quick on the uptake: Irish impatience under blinding blarney veneer. "Hurry it up, will you!" Lavishly proud of his city. Lived there all his life. Still lives there, all dressed up, talking about the big blue bay.

And Ebersprecher. Zoltan Ebersprecher. Wibaux, Montana. "That's not too far from here." A master belcher. Could also bugle like an elk and walk long distances on his hands. A hundred and fifty pushups. Always singing "Cecilia" with a theatrical lisp. Became an engineer. Dropped dead in Denver, Colorado.

"What about Zook?" Zook died two-three years ago. He went back to Cleveland after the war. A perpetual squint. Dennis Albemarle Zook. Crazy for baseball. Worked for some big department store. Laughed at the drop of a hat. Went back during the landing at St. Lo and pulled some leg-shot kid out of the water and got him up on shore. Saved his life.

"I thought that was Jones."

"No, that was Zook."

"I could have sworn it was Jones."

"I'm pretty sure it was Zook."

Zook or Jones. Maybe Jones, probably Zook. Winner take all the cicada shells.

They had finally covered it all as best they could and got up from their chairs. Donald Hanks had cooled in the recollection; his big face was shiny but dry. Eldon took him for a little walk around the place, showed him the two horses with dream-spittle on their lips and the single pink hollyhock beside the gate. There was a clothesline with denims on it and an abandoned pit toilet with an elm sapling growing out from under it. He showed Donald a pile of deer skulls along the fence, then nodded toward a swale in the adjoining field.

"I had two sons lived over there. One and then the other. Eldon Junior and then Everett. They were good boys but they took to drinking. One of them got drunk one night and let the house burn down around him. Couple of years later Everett put a house up there. The same thing happened to him about six months later. Two fires in one place." He turned back toward the house.

"I'm awful sorry to hear it, Eldon."

"After that happened I almost forgot all about the war."

Donald went to his rented car before he drove away and got a video camera from the backseat. He asked his friend to stand outside the kitchen door. He shot Eldon for a full minute standing uneasily with his arms hanging limp and his eyes off over the fence somewhere. Donald panned slowly to the left, getting the rest of the house, the two chairs in deep shadow, and then the horses asleep on their feet and the valley where the road ran beyond. A pause, then back slowly across the house to Eldon, who hadn't moved a muscle, and on to the right, the other half of the yard with the outhouse, the old wooden fence, lagged a moment at the field where the boys had burned, the gentle lift of the grassland and yucca above—then on out, panning to the hills southeast, sweeping the whole half-circle, slowly across the heat-shimmied southern skyline, the southwest with a trace of the Cannonball visible way off, and back, bearing back in, the horses again, the edge of the sky-blue house, Eldon, with one hand now in a hip pocket.

*****

One of the men by the haystack got up to go home. The heat of the day was breaking. Eldon and the other old man, the man who had seen the ghost smoking at the bridge, sat a while longer. They had known each other since 1922.

"Did you hear about Mickey Mouse getting a divorce from Minnie? He said she was fucking Goofy."

Yesterday Eldon had thought about the war. Not much at all today. Less the war than kind Donald Hanks who had come all the way from Atlanta, Georgia, with a good bit of it stuck in his teeth.

Eldon was pretty sure it was Zook pulled that boy on shore. And just then, right through the Minnie Mouse joke, he was remembering a split second of the day he got back from it all, a welcome-home parade down at Fort Yates, not too far from here. There was a brief dusty scuffle: A dog nipped a child. A band with two tubas was playing.

II. An August Third

I stopped at the high point of the hump road—a solitary breezy place I was fond of on the gravel road crossing the Porcupine–Wounded Knee divide. I got out to stretch and go to the bathroom in the ruddy bluestem and look at the Black Hills off to the west.

Early that morning I had pulled in to a desolate ranch house a hundred miles to the south to ask directions among the unpredictable back roads. It was a lovely site tucked against a protective rise. An elderly woman answered my knock, a petite pink-cheeked lady in an apron, a sweet American Swede with uplifted eyes working diligently through thick glasses. She invited me in. Soon we were seated, the two of us, at her lacy dining room table. She brought me a saucer of cookies and a tall glass of milk and told me her story: her early homestead life on that very ground (a tractor shed out back had been their dugout home the first several years); the premature death of her first husband; the sad unraveling and slow demise of a second, leaving her twice alone there. She began to weep, daubing with an ironed hanky at her nose. Then I caught it and began to choke up with my mouth full of macaroon—and then we pulled ourselves together. She advised me on my route and we said good-bye. But I thought of her more than once that day and stopped the car and stretched and threw imaginary fastballs.

"Are you choking your chicken?!"

By the time I turned and located the voice through the sun the men were laughing. It was a good surprise. They were back in the shade of cherry bushes in a sharp ravine below me. They were all chuckling as I walked down the grassy slope to see them.

The heat was like a slurry in the air. But these men were experts. Their cherry patch was situated at the head of the ravine, just where it first split the hillside open. I had to scramble down three feet to get in under its shade. And there they sat in the almost shocking cool of their shelter. It had the feel of a hut or a lair; there was plenty of headroom and elbow room. Chokecherries dangled around the edges. The men's expertise meant they sat erect and alert, neither sleeping nor restless. I knew John Door. One of the others had a jug of shadow-cool tea. We all wore faded wash-worn shirts with thin spots and bramble tears in them. We all shook hands.

Below the cherry patch the ravine dropped and deepened between steep white walls. Ash trees and dark cedars grew from its narrow floor, and farther down tall cottonwoods on their tiptoes, their crowns brushing and just breaking the upper coulee walls. It was dense and sunless as a cave. From down there somewhere a man called out in a hoarse voice, then I could make out people stirring in a cedar's shadow maybe thirty yards below us.

"They're drinking down there," John said. "You should have been here the other day. It was real hot. We were sitting here and all of a sudden this big fancy car comes over the hump, just rolling along, and then it pulls over real fast—right up there where you stopped. There was a man and a woman in it and they jumped out and started peeling off their clothes and then they crawled in the backseat together. They were in a big hurry. They must have been awful hot around the collar." The other men chuckled affirmatively. "It was a big Cadillac or something like that. I don't know where they were from. They had blue license plates. Joe says Iowa."

Another day they had seen a car stop and a priest get out and drop to his knees in the thin grass and pray with his clasped hands extended up and his head thrown back as in the Gethsemane illustrations. It was a provocative road.

We heard a coarse grunt and a brief thrashing of limbs. A large man was making his way up the ravine toward us. He was having a time of it, helping himself along with saplings, and when he arrived he was winded and stood heaving for a good while, casting long breakers of beer breath over us.

I had seen him before, more than once. I didn't really know him, but I remembered him well. He was a corpulent, noticeable man about sixty. Most of his days were spent loitering conspicuously, helplessly, in public places—gas stations, grocery store entryways, post offices—with his trousers sagging and his shirttails flying loose. He was desperately social, yet socially formless and chameleonic in a needy omnivorous way. He stood season after season, moist-lipped, watching orphanlike and longingly up and down the streets. But when he was drinking he had a notorious mean and manipulative side to him. Enough so that most people called him "Haywire." He had mastered the aggressive whine and the surly kowtow. He was given to using the prehistoric past as a sort of scenic, penny ante and lucrative leverage. One day in front of the grocery I overheard him working on a white couple with cameras around their necks; he had one arm around the man's shoulders and was going on in a lugubrious voice about his hard-pressed ancestors planting beans along the Missouri River a thousand years ago. The woman had tears in her eyes.

And now he stood holding onto a cherry branch, staring at me with a breathless, bruised St. Bernard look on his face. John skillfully tried to distract him, prodded him with brisk empty repartee. The other men were obviously uneasy in his presence; among other things, if he lost his balance and toppled down the hill he might well take a good part of the cherry patch with him. Finally he said something. "This woman goes to the doctor. Comes home and tells her husband everything is OK. He says, 'What about your big fat ass?' She says, 'Your name wasn't even mentioned.'" He fastened an open-mouthed glower on me for a long moment, then went back down the hill.

We sat talking. Now and then the jug of tea went around. The floor of the cherry patch was comfortable, picked clean and worn soft by the layering of summer days. The men hung their caps on the same twig-pegs every day. The afternoon relaxed and uncoiled. I realized this was what I had wanted to do all day. It was better than river driving, better than bank fishing. It had a sensible side-step dignity to it that made it seem ingenious-under-fire.

Haywire bellowed down below. We knew it was directed more or less our way. Seconds later he bellowed again and John reached behind him for a paper bag and pulled out sandwiches for all of us. It was some sort of lunch meat and cheese. The whole thing was saturated with a virulent and cloying perfume.

"Who made these?" I asked him.

"Aida. She made them before she went to work. She works at the government office. She gets all dressed up and wears lots of perfume."

"*Whew.* They're good though."

While we ate, John began telling me about a local incident that people were following. A religious man on the reservation had agreed to instruct three Caucasians in a vision quest. They planned it all carefully. They were going up on Bear Butte, doing it right. They would fast for four days. This all happened about two weeks ago.

He was interrupted by the big man—we heard him thrashing in the understory and then he was coming up the hill. He was drunker by now, more surly. Maybe he smelled the sandwiches. He took hold of a cherry branch and stared at me. The other men shifted and cleared their throats. I felt responsible for this unpleasant burr in a lazy, temperless day and wished Haywire were far away in some other well-insulated ravine. He addressed me in a lathery voice:

"Sioux chief and white general meet out on the prairie to smoke the peace pipe. Chief smokes, passes the pipe to the general. General takes out his handkerchief and wipes off the mouthpiece, then smokes. He gives the pipe back to the Indian. Chief takes out his knife and cuts off the mouthpiece, throws it away. General says, 'Why did you do that? White men are clean, Indians are dirty.' The chief says, 'No way. You're the dirty ones. Indians go to the bathroom outside. White man shits in his own house. I blow my nose on the grass. You blow your snot in a rag and carry it around in your pocket. You ruined my best pipe.' "

Then he slid back down to his friends in the cedars.

The tea went around. John resumed his desultory tale. The three vision questers had given the Sioux religious man 200 dollars apiece. All three bought expensive buffalo robes from a man in Rapid City. The religious man put them in a sweat lodge, then took them up on the side of Bear Butte and got them situated in a propitious spot. They talked for a while and prayed and smoked. Then the religious man left them alone. Said he would come back for them in four days.

Haywire was roaring down below. I envisioned him fumbling to load a .30-.30 with wild plum pits. Joe stepped out of the patch and walked off a civilized measure to go to the bathroom. A pickup truck slowed on the gravel berm; its dustcloud drifted through it and away. A boy yelled from the near window: "Is Morris in there?" John told him no, he hadn't seen him today.

"So after four days the men are waiting on the butte. They hadn't had anything to eat for the whole time. And the religious man didn't show up. They waited and waited. He never showed up. Finally they walked down by themselves."

Someone else was scrambling up the slope from the cedars now— a slim little man wearing cowboy boots outside of his jeans. He was grinning an enthusiastic grin and told us a quick joke about mothballs, you know what they smell like? and how did you get their little legs apart? and walked off toward the road. John yelled after him, "What's Haywire doing?"

"He's passed out," the man answered over his shoulder. "He's passed out cold." It was good news close at hand, a minor victory for the durability of the day. We all recrossed our legs and got comfortable.

"Those three men didn't have their car or anything. They went to a ranger station and finally got a ride into Sturgis where they had parked. They asked everyone they saw about the religious man. Nobody knew anything. The three men began to get mad. Six hundred dollars. After they rested up and had something to eat they drove down here and started looking for that medicine man. They went to his house. Nobody knew where he was; he hadn't been there for several days. They went to Pine Ridge, went to the tribal office. They even went down to Nebraska to the bars looking for him. They were getting madder and madder. Nobody had seen that man for days. He was just gone. Gone somewhere with the money. … Joe says Santa Fe."

The episode had overnight become a bit of local folklore: The three men prowling the reservation in search of the medicine man, their candy-red car with ski racks on it—every day or so people saw it somewhere between Wanblee and Oglala, driving slowly and watchfully along the roads, or parked in amateurish surveillance behind a barn.

Haywire and apparently all his comrades were sleeping; there was a cushiony silence from the lower ravine. A hawk went by, glinted in a lessened light: The afternoon was fading, falling away. No one talked for half an hour. Piñon jays were stirring, crying somewhere up on the shady side of the ridge.

Joe looked at me with a savvy new-phase-of-the-moon look on his face. "You should come with us. We're going over to White Horse Creek for a feast. A cattle truck ran off the road over there last night, rolled off that steep hill. The driver told the people over there they could shoot all the cattle that were hurt. Now they're throwing a feed for everyone."

Day makes night. I drove. I could still taste the wild perfume on my teeth. I would have whistled something from *Aida* if I knew it. It was an evening—the very word—an evening whose sky in an hour would have that untouchable cool-down melon color streaming through its trees; you could see it coming. And I was with experts. We were headed for kettles of beef simmering on cottonwood fires. There would be tubs of canned corn and macaroni salad. Poor-wills calling. Under a moth-battered yardlight, a card table of frosted yellow flatcakes. Urns of coffee. John said I could always sleep at his place.

III. Bacon, Flour, Sugar, Tree

LeTurner was always a nook and cranny man. He required a fundamental privacy: As a boy he had run off from the reservation boarding school ten times. It was a state record by a hair. They always found him a day or two later in deep, fey concentration—as if he didn't see them standing there looking grimly down at him—in some little known nook or pine-needled cranny near the family home. And this day seventy years later he was in out of the sun below a twenty-foot cottonwood, sitting in a slight hollow in the grassy glacis. It was an uncertain tree, dog-legged and slight of crown, its midday shadow was modest for two grown men, but they managed, LeTurner and another man, an approximate peer in things north-central Montanan, and squinted out over the plain.

It was a hot day. Twenty years ago, maybe even five years ago, LeTurner would have walked up the slope on the slalom a mile or so into the cool pines that sprang up there and continued black and aromatic up across the flanks of the Little Rockies. But now he was too old and so was the other and they sat happy enough near the Fort Belknap road in the shade of the tree with a blanched church sign nailed to it. There was a dead porcupine on the edge of the road, and then the sharp blue shadows of the Judith Mountains on the skyline eighty miles southwest.

They hadn't known one another more than two or three years. They began running into each other along this road and then began to share the shade of the cottonwood when hot days caught them together and they had no other destinations. They sat and spoke of little gnat-like things. LeTurner was a small wiry man. If people looked twice at him it was to verify his bandy bowlegs or the fancy yellow flicker feather in his hat. He said little, kept his teeth clenched with his full lips hanging open, and was partial to Sen-Sen candy.

The other man had heard a story about LeTurner, just a murmur, but enough to catch his ear, of a sharp-edged incident far off behind him, long-finished but notable—less than some, more than others. Just a muddy whisper of it—but the facts of the matter were that in the summer of 1928 with Calvin Coolidge at the helm LeTurner Lake and his wife and baby were living happily in a little Indian town, in a pleasant cabin-house on the windward side of these mountains; they looked up and saw them every day. It was a town of twelve or fifteen homes set on dirt streets with an occasional hard-pressed tree. LeTurner was eighteen. He did wage work on nearby ranches and came home and played with his child. His wife was a good-looking woman with thin shanks and fine long hair. She worked two or three days a week up in Demo Crossing, a mixed-blood and white town eight miles north. She cleaned house up there for a half-breed man who ran a mercantile and made good money and smoked thin crooked cigars and stood around with his thumbs hooked in his pantwaist.

In the latter half of July 1928, the merchant began to tumble for the woman. He was a one-eyed man called Borgne. His squinting gave him an on-running harsh grimace, but he was really a harmless, moony sort of man. And he fell for the girl. He watched her all day long, followed her from room to room, tried to talk with her while she worked. This went on for several weeks. People in Demo began to notice the way the merchant stared at her and followed her into the yard while she beat the rugs and shook the blankets.

Then one day he showed up down in the woman's cabin town on one of her days off. He pulled his Model A off the road and got out and leaned against the car, smoking a cigar and gazing at the woman's house. Then he drove away. But people saw him, that time and the next, and began to sense what was going on, and the more he drove down there the more they began to get nervous.

LeTurner had no inkling what was going on until his brother called him over one afternoon and said, "I think that Borgne man up in Demo is sniffing around your wife." LeTurner asked his wife about it when she got home that night. She said the merchant was looking at her all the time, but she didn't think there would be any trouble. LeTurner sat and pictured the dusty streets of that town eight miles north, just barely there, with the trees of the big river at its far edge, and wagons tied at the curbs.

That night most all the residents of LeTurner's community knew that a car pulled up along the road and sat there a long while in the dark with its engine running. Next morning at first light LeTurner walked over to the place and found two black cigar butts ground out in the dirt. That Borgne hadn't sense enough even to cover them up as any decent dog would have.

LeTurner told his wife to wait for him in the cabin, then walked over to his brother's house at the edge of the village. His brother was in the yard drinking coffee with a tiny new pup riding in his shirt pocket. He helped LeTurner put the team to the wagon and watched him drive away.

LeTurner took the old low road north. It was rough and dusty, paralleling the newer high road about half a mile west of it. The two routes joined about a mile below Demo Crossing where a store and gas station stood, its new planking still bright raw in the morning sun. The merchant Borgne wasn't home, LeTurner saw his big car was gone and the doors shut up tight. An old man on the street told him the merchant had taken his Model A out to the dump with a load of cans. LeTurner found him there, just sweeping out his backseat with a whisk. The merchant stopped and watched the wagon coming up pretty fast. When LeTurner set the brake and climbed down with his rifle the merchant looked at him like a hound in a tight corner, but then something changed and he stood up straight and tall as if he were getting his picture taken, and that's the way he was when LeTurner shot him.

LeTurner drove back on the high road. He pulled the wagon up before his door and pretty soon he and his wife were loading their belongings. They didn't hurry. They wrapped things right and stowed them securely in the wagon bed. In an hour they were ready and drove calmly out. His brother walked them to the big road with one hand on the wagon rail; he was still carrying the red and white pup in his shirt pocket.

They drove south twelve miles and then cut up a shadowy mining trail and climbed into the Little Rockies. They followed a small stream up, crossed a low pass through the cooked-out end-of-summer pines. They weren't running. They weren't in a hurry. They had everything they owned right with them. By late afternoon they reached a narrow valley in the eastern half of the range, a pretty place with no one around and red willows along its creek. They slept under the wagon and next morning put up a wall tent and made a tentative camp with the tent stakes not hammered in all the way and set their minds to waiting and seeing.

Three weeks went by, they were into a sweet September, and nothing had happened—no sheriff and deputies rode over the hill. Three weeks. LeTurner didn't know what to think. This place wasn't much of a secret to anybody around here. He wondered why nothing had happened by now. He shot a deer. The first quick snow blew through. And then he decided to go back over the mountain and find out what was going on.

He traveled openly, calmly, but timed things so that he arrived at his brother's house just after dark. He could see them in the lighted kitchen sitting around the table with the litter of pups wrestling on the floor. He stood inside the door and talked quietly with his brother. "What's going on back here? Nobody ever came after us. Did the Borgne man die?"

Two cousins had come over to the house by now.

"He died. He died right away. They buried him over at Havre, that's all I know."

LeTurner asked his brother to go with him to the gas station up the north road and see if they could learn anything. They took the wagon with a young brother-in-law riding in the back. LeTurner pulled the team up off to one side and sent his brother in to buy tobacco. "Make sure he really died." He could see him inside standing by the counter talking with the proprietor, another half-breed man heavy on the Cree side, and a knowledgeable loiterer a bony akimbo near the crackling stove.

He was back in a quarter hour, standing beside the wagon wheel in the dark telling LeTurner what he heard. LeTurner sat sideways in the seat with the reins wrapped around one thigh.

"He died right away. I told you that. They buried him over in Havre."

"What's that sheriff been doing about it?"

"Nobody knows anything about the sheriff."

"Seems like he'd be after me by now if that Borgne died."

"Seems like he would. Maybe he heard you were gone to Canada."

"Maybe he did."

"Ernie said someone was saying you might be down in Riverton, Wyoming."

"Who said that?"

"I don't know. Somebody just talking about it. Nobody told any lies."

The loiterer left the station and walked away and the screen door finally slammed behind him. The brothers drove home and LeTurner slept on the floor for a couple of hours and then started back to his wife in the mountains.

He still didn't know what to think, and neither did his wife, but after another week they began to firm up the camp. They cut firewood and insulated the tent and one day the brother showed up with the provisions LeTurner had requested: sugar and flour and bacon and tea. They were almost forgetting about the sheriff and the town. They were in out of the wind, and then it was spring and the woman was heavy with child again, and they decided to turn some ground near the creek and plant beans and corn.

And the sheriff never came over the hill. LeTurner went back to Demo once more and talked a little in the nightfall and bought a sack of flour. He wondered now and then how a thing like that could happen and cast no shadow. He wondered what had happened to the State of Montana and the United States of America under Franklin Roosevelt and even the Dominion of Canada and the Mounties, if that's where they thought he went.

And that was the only thing he ever shot, that and a hundred deer. The next summer the brother and some in-laws helped them put up a cabin in the valley and the following spring a cousin moved down there and built one and there were children yelling around the place and wood smoke in the air.

A car slowed and stopped along the highway where the old men were sitting. A younger fellow got out and opened the trunk and began carving a big watermelon in there. He carried two thick slices across the ditch and up to the shade of the little cottonwood. The old men were happy to see it. They ate and spat the seeds starboard. The young man offered them a ride home. But it was too early to go home, too hot.

The little settlement camp in the mountains is still there, although LeTurner left it years ago when his wife died during the Eisenhower administration. Twenty or thirty people live there, grandchildren, great grandchildren, ravens overhead. Even a place to buy soda pop in the summer. Fifty years ago, as people started settling there, they called the place LeTurner, but LeTurner wasn't easy with that, thought it was pushing his luck, so they called it "Osier" after the creek running there. Nowadays they say it "O-seer." It's eighteen and a half miles as the crow flies from the foot of the cottonwood tree.

Borgne's people are all long gone to Havre and beyond. The sheriff is dead for quite a while and his people gone to Spokane and Boise, long gone. The town where the shooting took place has almost disappeared. The wind has it, plays with it like a cat.

Pie for Breakfast

From the café counter I was watching a boy out back plinking at something up in a tree with his air rifle. I hadn't slept well—it was deer season in eastern Montana and the high school girls drove by the little motel until what seemed the middle of the night, honking and bluff-whistling at the out-of-town hunters gathered in the parking lot. I watched the boy in patched baggy jeans and a brown jacket fire his BB gun nearly straight up in the air and then stand there with his mouth open as if he were waiting to catch a high-lobbed piece of popcorn.

Then I ordered bacon and eggs and a slice of pie, and the young man down the counter did exactly the same, and we began to talk.

"I haven't seen a true lemon pie in ten years."

I knew Ida hadn't made the pie as soon as I saw it sitting on the serve-up. It was too generously full and too fancy around the edges. She set down her cigarette and leaned through the cook's window and told us her sister was visiting and she had made Ida three pies to earn her keep.

It was a wonderful pie, the kind with whole unpeeled lemons in it, sliced thin as paper and cooked with lots of sugar and eggs into a custardy mass. Ida said her sister would only mix it in a yellow bowl. The man at the counter liked it too, and around his last forkful told me about a fresh fig pie he had run into in California, another custard-style pie with chopped figs in it, served cold. He had a small notebook on the counter and carried half a dozen ball-point pens in his shirt pocket.

A pair of very old men came shuffling into the place, talking loudly. They were bent-up and deaf and slow on their feet, but it was obvious they were longtime friends and they were immensely happy to be out together. A boy was with them, keeping an eye and moving obstacles from their path. It might have been the boy who was shooting the air rifle. The two men sat side by side along one wall and conversed in hoarse intimate shouts.

I was telling the man at the counter about a cider pie I had sampled once in New England, an honest-enough, timberless pie, and Ida came out front with smoke twirling from her nostrils and talked about the transparent pies of northern Kentucky, from up along the Ohio River, and I remembered a cane syrup pie I picked up at a bake sale near Thibodaux, Louisiana.

A UPS driver and a ranch couple were now in the café. One of the old men was bellowing gleefully into his cohort's ear: I WAS OVER COURTING THIS GIRL ONE AFTERNOON. WE WERE SITTING ON THE PORCH AND I SAW AN OLD TABBY CAT OUT ON THE LAWN WASHING ITS FACE REAL NICE AND I SAID TO THE GIRL "I BET THAT CAT'S DOING SOMETHING YOU HAVEN'T DONE TODAY" AND BY THE TIME SHE LOOKED OVER THERE THE CAT HAD TURNED AROUND AND HIKED ITS LEG AND WAS LICKING ITS HINDER.

And the young man at the counter was going on about chess pie, how it should be made only with buttermilk, and that if you go far south and add a handful of chopped dates to chess pie you've got Jeff Davis pie. Then he jumped, understandably, to Robert E. Lee cake, a lemony yellow cake layered with a lemon curd filling and served cool, out on the veranda.

We got up to leave together. The two old men were still wiping their eyes and blowing their noses after the tabby cat story. The UPS man had wolfed his eggs and gone. I asked Ida how long her sister would be with her, just for reference on the pie futures in case I got through town again soon.

In the parking lot I noticed the man had boxes of books and tabulation in his backseat. A geologist? Anthropologist.

"I'm working on a project around here. Something that's never been done before, as far as I know. I'm doing a study on what you might call White Indians."

I shaded my eyes with one hand.

"I mean people who really jump into it, pretty much give up their own cultures, move west and settle on a reservation. I'm interested in how they go about it. How they penetrate, what happens deep down in their private lives, their language, their daily habits, the works. I'm locating people now and want to stay in touch with them for a period of years, follow up on them.

"The last time I was over here I interviewed a woman living in a cabin up north. She's about twenty-five. From Philadelphia. She was mashing chokecherries with a stone hammer, drying meat in the sun. She was making pemmican. Hadn't been off the reservation in two years."

"No pie."

"No pie."

"Have you met the kid over around Lame Deer, a blond kid with braids?"

"No." He had his notebook and one of his pens out.

"You might want to talk to him. He dresses 1865 every day of the year. Leggings, breechcloth, otter braidwraps. I don't know his name, but he's not hard to find. Look for him in front of the big grocery store on the highway. Or south of town, down by the powwow grounds. I see him down there a lot, sitting back along the creek by himself."

Northbound Bus

A man named Williams opened a coffeehouse a few blocks off the main street in Cheyenne, Wyoming. The coffee was good and strong; there was an espresso machine at the ready, and a chessboard folded on the counter with the playing pieces in an old White Owl cigar box. Williams wanted the place to be the real thing, a place for thought and discussion and perhaps, eventually, free verse aloud. But he was realistic enough to simmer a cauldron of soup each morning and lay a bed of submarine sandwiches in a case by the door to sell to neighborhood workers. After a while some of the railroad crews began to walk the extra blocks to fill their big Thermoses with mocha java or minestrone for the long haul to Omaha.

But it wasn't a lunch place, he insisted, no luncheonette or diner. It was a coffeehouse in the grand tradition. Williams played long-running tapes of Stan Getz or Thelonius Monk and kept a volume of Carl Sandburg on the premises and a stack of stale *Village Voices* on the tables as cloudseed.

It was a heroic struggle, wrangling up the thought and conversation, until the retired doctor discovered the establishment and began to frequent it late mornings for an hour or two before he walked home and turned his afternoon attention to liquor by the large glass.

The doctor was an intelligent, humor-blessed man who could keep up with Williams in intellectual banter, and he seemed to answer the coffeekeeper's ultimate prayer. Dr. Todd had been a physician in Denver for thirty years, a good physician and a gentle man, until the drinking cost him everything. In the end, his wife took the two teenaged children back to Illinois. Then he lost his driver's license forever after a series of humiliating car accidents that left him sitting uncomprehendingly in the shallows of Cherry Creek or far up on a Blake Street sidewalk surrounded by drifts of shattered glass. And soon he lost his practice as well, gave it all up, sold his big brick house on Gilpin Street and retreated to a cozy bungalow in Cheyenne, Wyoming, to get by and drink in primitive peace. During the cold months he sipped Old Crow bourbon beside a sunny window; summers he drank iced Smirnoff vodka and nibbled saltines on the shady side of the house. He switched beverages each spring and fall with a minor ceremony on the day the clocks were changed for daylight savings.

He was lonely, and often sad, but remarkably steady in his new life. Once, sometimes twice, a year he took long solitary bus rides for diversion. At first his destinations were solid: the Ozarks in autumn, an art tour in Santa Fe. Then they became trips for their own sake, for the reliable panoramic passage of landscape and the inevitable sociality of the passengers on the bus. To Kansas City and back. A round-trip on the San Francisco Scenicruiser Express with a flask in each pocket and a mystery novel on his lap.

So when the man Williams opened the coffeehouse the doctor was delighted. Every morning, they managed, the two of them, to mount some sort of brisk discussion accompanied by Herbie Mann or Lester Young. Williams usually set the topic: international affairs, political mire, speculative philosophy. The Irish Republican Army. Ancient Roman mores. The death of Andy Warhol. They went at it like badminton, and they managed quite well. Now and then a secretary or a Union Pacific brakeman joined in. On days when the doctor was sluggish and bleary from the previous day's drink, Williams would skillfully urge him, prod him steadily into the topic until the doctor came around, joining in with a "Touché!" or "That's exactly the point!" and dialogue was attained.

One day in the fall of the year—it was scarcely a week since he had switched from vodka to bourbon—the doctor announced that he was taking a trip to Montana, to Billings, Montana, to look up a distant cousin. He had a ticket on the Powder River line and he pulled it out to show Williams. Dr. Todd hadn't seen his second cousin Betty in several decades, or even heard much from her of late. But he preferred not to telephone ahead, he explained. Why sabotage a perfectly good bus ride? If she wasn't there he would enjoy a steak dinner at a nice restaurant and come home.

He boarded the 10 a.m. bus at the Cheyenne depot and was pleased to find it crowded with passengers who must have got on in Denver. He felt a mild wave of nostalgia for his former home city and took an aisle seat toward the rear of the bus. An Indian boy slept soundly against the window.

The bus rolled north for half an hour before it began to make the local stops. Chugwater. Wheatland. Dropping the occasional stiff pilgrim or taking up heavily-taped pasteboard freight. It was monotonous on a cloudy day when the colors were down. The Indian boy slept deeply. The doctor had a nip of Old Crow to keep him company. When the bus stopped in Douglas for a 40-minute lunch break, the doctor hesitated, then gently nudged the boy and told him it was time to eat.

In the café next door to the depot, the waitresses were cynically braced for the daily lunch-bus hubbub. The doctor ordered the noon special, roast pork and sweet potatoes, and carried it to a table and sat beside the Indian boy and his cheeseburger. The food strengthened Dr. Todd and he began to chat. "Pork and yams.... I believe I could enjoy life in the South Pacific on one of those islands where they raise nothing but hogs and sweet potatoes. That would suit my fancy." He told the boy about butchering day back in the Illinois of his youth, told how they set aside the little tenderloins (they called them the "fish") from each hog, and then, at mealtime, dropped them whole into a kettle of hot lard and ate them under an October maple tree. The boy thought, "Oh shit, this man is telling me his life story."

But the doctor wasn't telling his life story. That was the last story he wanted to tell. Back on the Powder River bus, when they were back on the highway, he asked the boy's name.

"Orlen."

"Orlen."

"Orlen Bay Horses."

"Orlen Bay Horse. That's a fine name."

"Horses."

"Bay Horses. That's a wonderful name. My name is Thomas Todd.... I have always admired those grand family names you hear of now and then. Trueheart. Greathouse. Lovejoy. Even Armstrong. It seems to me it would be easier to move through life with a name like that to ride on. It seems it would keep the wind in your sails. Goodfellow is another one. And I knew a boy with the name of Birdsong. I always wanted to trade him, even up: Todd for Birdsong. That would have been a deal."

They paused in Glenrock and the city of Casper and the village of Kaycee. The doctor gazed appreciatively, elegiacally, from the window. Every now and again he took a discreet sip of bourbon, and occasionally commented on something to the boy, and later presented him with one of the ball-point pens in his shirt pocket. They could see the Bighorns out the left-side windows by now, with the evening sun raying out over them. Somewhere north of Buffalo there was a house in the dusky foothills with colored Christmas lights glittering on its eaves and lawn cedars.

"They're a little early this year aren't they?"

The boy looked out. "They're still up from last year I think. I see them like that every time I ride this bus."

The doctor was ordinarily adept at timing his liquor in public places. But this day, after the bus had departed Sheridan and full autumn dark fell, somewhere near the Montana border, he stepped up his sipping, finished the right pocket flask and began on the left, and the Bay Horses boy dozed, up through Lodgegrass and Crow Agency.

They pulled into Billings at 9:30. The doctor followed Orlen off the bus and into the bright lights of the station. A young man was waiting for Orlen, leaning against a whitewashed wall. The doctor had to stop and rest inside the door, set down his little gym bag on the floor. He was surprised to discover he was unsteady, even drunk. He had lost his timing and botched it.

He saw Orlen and his tall cousin begin to walk toward the door and he called after them. The boys came back to him shyly.

"I'm sorry, Orlen. I'm sorry to trouble you. I've had too much, I regret to say. 'Yo no soy puede mas.' Will you do something for me, Orlen? I'll pay you for it if you do. I'd like you to take this letter to my cousin. It's got some old family photos in it. She lives here in Billings, the address is on the envelope. But I've had too much. I think I'll take the next bus back to Cheyenne. Will you do it for me, Orlen?"

The boys glanced at each other. It was a clear-cut fifty-fifty proposition. Doctor Todd fished out two ten-dollar bills and held them out to Orlen. The boy considered for a moment, reached out and took one of the bills.

"This will be enough."

The doctor slept in a bus station chair and then caught the midnight bus back south. He spent a full 24 hours in bed when he got home. But the following day, after an especially slow and hearty breakfast (he opened a tin of kippered fish to go with his scrambled eggs and sliced tomatoes), he walked gratefully the half dozen blocks to the coffeehouse. He peeked in the window and saw that the tables were empty. Williams turned from his soup cauldron when he heard the door.

"Hail Atlantis! I missed you, Doc. How's Betty?"

Cold Hands, High Water

Like many American highways, know it or not, that stretch of interstate in central Wyoming has a shadow route paralleling it, a worn, way-of-least-resistance pedestrian trail a hundred yards to one side, like a secretive towpath along a canal, between Billings and Denver. The uncowed penniless, the shy underbelly, and restless minstrels use it.

I was stopped there at a pretty place on the bank of the Laramie River, a tree-lined semiprivate mile of valley in early summer. A river couldn't cut a better place. I pitched my tent and hid my bicycle in a willow brake as soon as I saw the spot.

It had been an abnormally wet spring. The valley hills shone with an aggressive, almost crayon green; throughout the day you could see the white rumps of pronghorns bright against the skyline grass. Cattle feasted in the bottomland on the other side of the river, up to their fetlocks in water, then dozed sated among the pale Russian olive groves. The new Hereford calves looked like gleaming buckeyes fresh from the shells.

I was washing up my plate and skillet the next morning when I saw a man coming along the footpath. He was approaching from the north, the same way I had ridden in the day before. He was a young fellow with a rucksack on his back and a flyrod case over one shoulder. He walked right up as if he were expected.

He spoke a careful, well prepared European English that immediately slowed everything down luxuriantly; his sentences reminded me of a waiter carrying a heavily loaded tray. He had come from Denmark ten days before, he told me, to fish the American West. And after half a decade of planning and daydreaming and setting aside money, he had chosen the Wet Year to buy his ticket. The wildflowers were everywhere extravagant, but all the rivers were unfishably high. He told the tale with a clownish cast, but I could see it was a sad one for him. He had spent most of his money desperately riding buses from stream to swollen stream. He had just hitchhiked despondently down from the Bighorn.

I had a tin of Spam and a can of white beans. We built a small fire and fried slices of the meat and then poured in the beans. The meal cheered him a little. We ate oranges and talked and I began to realize how deeply he was disheartened, rocked, by his bad luck. When he wasn't talking, balancing that precarious English tray, he was obviously flogged, laid out like a peony bush after a storm.

So when he dozed off under the olive tree I wrote a quick note and bicycled the three or four miles south on the footpath to a highway interchange and bought a pint of California brandy in the hamlet there and pedaled back to camp. I finally found him, spotted his vertical, extenuated shape, in the shade of an ash tree. Good God, I thought, he's hung himself. Then, as I approached, he broke the tableau, laughing, pulled the loose rope from the ash limb and walked to greet me with a broad smile on his face. I took it as an official release from pity or concern.

He had five days before he caught the train in Denver, so he stayed there on the Laramie with me. He seemed to like the place as much as I did. The highway was mostly invisible from there; we heard the occasional truck roar by. No one bothered us. One afternoon a man in a slouch hat walked by going north, carrying a dapper valise.

The Dane stood looking at the river a good bit, and cast a few times to keep in practice, and each morning he borrowed my bicycle and rode to the highway to telephone a ranger station here or there and check on the various riverflows: the North Platte, the Cache la Poudre. But he was essentially resigned to no fishing in the American West. We ate rice and spaghetti and oranges and took hikes up valley to the point where ranches came into view. He was reading *Trout* by Ray Bergman and spoke frequently of his wife back home. She was a nurse in the National Orphanage, with blond hair trailing down her back. Next time she would come with him. He faithfully sent her postcards describing his days with subtle, poetic equivocation. And each afternoon, sooner or later I would return to camp from a stroll or from the latrine to find him in some sort of theatrical death scene, sprawled dramatically by the fire pit with one leg still twitching, or over on the bank of the stream with a grocery bag over his head. Then he would jump up smiling, brush off his short pants, and announce, "That was James Cagney in Such-and-such," or "The Last of the Romanovs!"

One day he showed me his packet of dry flies and nymphs, went through them one by one with great affection. "Henry's Fork only, this one. Tied by René Harrop."

"Do you know what you should do, Url?" He should get off the train, if he could arrange it, for a day or two in Ohio, call my friend Earley who lives there, and go fishing with him. It might still be smallmouth bass season out there. He could see those pretty, quiet streams I grew up with: gravel-bottomed, heavily shaded with real trees, with big oaks and beautiful sycamores. The Shawnee creeks we used to call them. Cool, dark, quiet, with young cornfields just beyond the river trees and the pewees calling. Those smallmouth will take the kinks out of your line, too. Earley could take him to some doozies in a couple of days.

He said it was a good idea. The next morning he got up early, did five minutes' worth of perfunctory calisthenics, and packed his gear for Denver. I showed him on the map where to go in Ohio and gave him Earley's phone number and three rice balls with chunks of Spam in them. We walked up to the rim of the valley together, then I turned back to camp. I cleaned the place up and started south that afternoon. It wasn't any fun anymore.

Three weeks later I called Earley out of itchy curiosity. Url had phoned him from some train station in western Iowa about one in the morning. They talked at length anyway, had actually made rather firm plans to fish a couple of days thereafter. Url had sounded enthusiastic, asked in great detail about the habits of the bass and what they might be hitting. I had a fleeting vision of him sprawled under an Ohio sugar maple: "Hector beneath the walls of Troy." But that was it. He never called again, never showed up on the banks of the Olentangy.

A Missouri Story

Two men strolled into Kansas City, Kansas. It was 1902 or 1903, an era when even most hoboes wore suits, and bowler hats as well if they hadn't blown off down the road and across the fields. These two men, both of them pedigreed Johnsons, wore dark dusty trousers but carried their dark dusty suitcoats over their shoulders. It was a hot midsummer day. The two were just off an accommodating freight train at the edge of town and stopped to drink long and deep at a spring pipe along the road.

They had been working the wheat harvest in western Kansas. They worked it, along with several dozen other hoboes, for two weeks at decent pay before Ferol, the small fellow, Ferol Johnson, had enough of the hard work and the chaff in the mouth and the shoes, and they quit. They had a few coins in their pockets and started east. Might as well go back to Chicago. They stopped along the way now and then to cut grass for a thin widow or wash windows for a square meal and a dime.

The two men had wandered together for eight months now, for no other good reason than that they were both Johnsons. Hiram, the large easygoing one with big palmetto hands, and Ferol, the skinny one with wiry yellow hair. A hobo on the train told them there was a Wobbly tent in KC, a place where men of the road could find a corner of shade and shelter, maybe a bowl of beans, maybe a speck of bacon in it. A place they could nap a day or two without worrying about a boot to the seat of their pants.

58

The Johnsons finally located the tent set up in a pasture near the river. They found a place under a tree where they loafed and talked with other hoboes as they drifted in or out. There was a blue sky and a south wind. At 5 o'clock there was a lecture in the tent, a man from the Hobo College in Chicago was going to give a talk. If you cared about your bowl of beans, it was recommended you attend.

The tent was full of men-on-the-move. Hiram found a seat and Ferol squeezed in the row behind him. The man from the college told a few pleasant stories and then delivered an address on the History of the Working Man Across the Ages. He spoke of Soil Turners and Stone Crushers and Capstan Gangs and bentbacked Navvies. Men whose inexpensive gravestones melted slowly but surely in the rain like tallow. Ferol had a sprig of bluestem grass and began to tickle Hiram with it on his neck. He sniggered when Hiram slapped politely at it for a mosquito a few times before he figured it out and finally snatched it out of Ferol's hand.

"Now you birds may not know it, but you birds, the working men, were the ones who made it all possible, made the growth and fabulous wealth of Europe possible. When the rich boys of Europe mastered the means of traveling the world and reaping its riches—America, Africa, Asia—who gave the rich boys, the business boys, the power to do it? You birds. You birds and your great-great-granddaddies. The businessmen had it all under control. They brought over coffee from South America, tea from China, tobacco from Virginia—For what? For cheap stimulants for the working man. Sugar from the Indies islands to keep him going. Potatoes from the New World to fill his belly cheap. Clothing, cheap clothing, woven from Mississippi cotton picked by the cheapest labor on earth, slave labor. Keep his belly full and his back covered and a pipe in his mouth. Cheap-cheap-cheap: That's you birds' song."

As they walked from the tent Hiram said, "You're a horsefly, Ferol. Your mother should've had the swatter after you." "She couldn't catch me, pard."

That night they slept on the ground near the tent and the next morning they took their time, lolling in the shade and enjoying the free coffee. Nobody jabbing them in the hinder with a sharp stick. They even met another Johnson. He spelled it with a "t": B.L. Johnston, but that was close enough. He had a lemon in his pocket, dried up like leather on the outside, but juicy on the in. He cut it up and gave Hiram and Ferol each a piece to suck on. "Oh mama."

The three of them left KC about noon. They got a ride on a farm wagon that carried them across the Missouri River and out northeast through the city. Hiram said he might as well show the boys his hometown of Hamilton, Missouri, on their way to Chicago. Nobody he knew was left there, but he'd like to see the old place.

The farmer took them up through Lawson and a few miles east, then dropped them off on a back road and they began to walk north. Blue sky, south wind full of dust and elderberry. Hiram and Ferol had their small blanket rolls of personal belongings over their shoulders. B.L. carried an old valise holding his razor and comb and the several tools he needed to ply his sporadic trade of umbrella repair. Ferol began to singsong a little chant as they moved along the hot road.

"Who's a Johnson? You's a Johnson. Me's a Johnson? He's a Johnson. Where's a Johnson? There's a Johnson. Why's a Johnson? I's a Johnson..."

When the sun got low the men decided to stop for the night and go on into Hamilton in the morning. They backtracked half a mile to a lonely old barn and slipped cautiously in through the unpainted door, looked around best they could in the dark, and made up their blanket beds in the haymow.

But someone saw them scuttle back the lane. It was hardly dark when two policemen and a pair of farmers rousted them out and looked them over by lantern light, searched their pockets and put them on a buckboard, drove them to the nearest little town. Elvira, Missouri, on a creek called Crooked Creek. They took them to the sheriff's office and the sheriff himself looked them over while he talked indignantly about the evil of tramps and the putrefaction of the national morale. "Take 'em down and tie 'em by the river overnight."

The police took the three down to a low field near the banks of the stream, ordered them to take off their shirts, and chained them standing up, with their arms stretched high, to a couple of maple trees and left them there. When they returned for them next morning the Johnsons were so riddled with mosquito bites their faces were swollen and their eyes puffed almost shut and their backs all torn up from trying to scratch themselves against the trees. The sheriff took them to the town square. It was Saturday, all the local farmers were in the village shopping. When they heard the sheriff was going to auction off some working men they gravitated to the square and leaned against their buggies and smoked in the early sun.

The sheriff stood up and led the Johnsons out in the open so the farmers could see them. "These boys are down on their luck and in search of fruitful employment, but just don't quite know how to go about it. I believe they have contracted a bad case of the Blind Staggers. So we are going to help them out of their predicament." He called up the farmer whose barn the Johnsons had trespassed and gave him first crack. The farmer looked them over and finally said, "I'll give two dollars a head for the big ones," and the sheriff said, "Sold American."

"What about the runt, Harold?"

"He wouldn't be worth his feed."

The sheriff walked among the crowd trying to find a buyer for Ferol. He finally offered him up for 75 cents, but nobody wanted him. The farmer who bought Hiram and B.L. already had them in the back of his wagon and was ready to drive off. They both turned around to look at Ferol when the team started up, and then they were gone. The sheriff eventually walked back to Ferol and told him he wasn't worth feeding and that he had ten minutes to get out of Elvira, Missouri, or he'd wish he had.

Ferol plucked up his scrawny blanket roll and hurried off. He could see brush and trees at the edge of town and started that way by instinct. Before he got there a band of schoolboys, egged on by their mothers in their doorways, began to pelt him with stones and taunt him down the shady little street. He broke into a bitter run and dove into the brushy ravine and hustled off along the creek. After a few minutes he stopped to listen back toward town. The mothers had called their boys in. Ferol caught his breath and made his way to a railroad trestle bridge and sat down under it. The damned mosquitoes were back again. The very sound of them made him sick to his stomach.

He knew he should get out of Missouri as soon as he could. But he was dead tired and he had the mosquito poison in him. So he let himself fall asleep on the cool dirt up under the bridge and slept a night's worth. When he awakened in the afternoon and the bugs got at him he went down to the stream and lay in it with just his nose out of water. At sundown a breeze picked up, there were clouds in the west. The wind kept the bugs down. He packed mud on his welted shoulders and back and slept another night's worth below heat lightning.

The next morning found him farther out the creek, lying in an Osage orange patch. He could see the old barn they had bedded in and off the other way the big white farmhouse with chickens in the yard and Guernsey calves behind it. It was Sunday morning, but the farmer had Hiram and B.L. out in a meadow and was standing solemnly in a good black suit watching them work. They were cutting a ditch across a broad field with ironweed and boneset in it. They must have started it yesterday as soon as they got there. Now they had paused for the first time to take their coats off and lay them on the ground. It was warming up early. Ferol had a blade of juicy grass in his teeth, chewing on it.

"Hell, those birds aren't doing anything I couldn't do."

Spanish For Vanish

Yesterday I stopped at the Belle Fourche post office to send off post cards. At the lobby counter beside me an elderly common man was struggling gamely to compose a letter on a small lined notepad. He murmured conversationally, word by word, as he wrote. It seemed to be a happy letter, though each phrase was a chore, each short paragraph a triumph that brought a twitch of smile to his lips. I believe he said, just as I was finishing up, "I dreamed about that old black dog one night."

*****

Each evening all week I sat with early English chamber music in the summer twilight, returned to it each evening for an hour or more without thought or question, nothing intended, sat with it and a nip of whiskey or a glass of wine. I began with some recent discoveries from the early 1600s: the Fantasia Suites of John Jenkins; plaintive, creaking-ship viol pieces by Thomas Lupo; odds and ends from Thomas Simpson, with crickets calling from beyond the door. Then reimmersed myself in the old favorites: Orlando Gibbons. John Dowland. The complete Royal Consort Suites of William Lawes, that foggy day half-jig, that saltwater and catgut insinuendo.

It turned into an experience of unexpected reach. The distinctive similarity of the various musics, the unbending strength of their conceded limits and agreed-upon tone, formed in the end a riverine channel of steady, utterly persuasive force. Rather than each standing alone as a voice in the wilderness, rather than diminishing one another by their mutual ground, the channelized style acted to deepen and enrich the whole to an extent that after five or six days the exposure was thorough enough that I began to sense within myself a simple working knowledge of 17th century Britain, an everyday familiarity as of my own world, an intimacy both unassuming and powerful. I had been unexpectedly rendered privy by artists firmly in milieu. John Coperario. Anthony Holborne. John Farmer. All facets were casually accounted for. I knew both treble and bass, winds from all quarters. I knew hanky and ha'penny, hawk overhead, bat in the gutter. It was a full-dress nonverbal infusion. I drank it in like a tonic I most obviously needed, and I was still braced and surprised by it this morning driving out from South Dakota.

When I first saw the man through the heat shimmy a quarter-mile off I figured he was a Sioux man hitchhiking down from the reservation, but at fifty yards I knew he wasn't. He climbed in the car, preferring to keep his gear handy at his feet. He was a pleasant-looking, darkish man in his twenties, I would guess. It was a hot northern Nebraska day by now, but he wore a bulky long-sleeved flannel shirt and thick trousers. His only luggage was a heavy wool blanket neatly rolled and tied and stuffed in a clear plastic bag. A tiny billed cap sat atop a head of dark and curly, nearly ringletted hair that looked almost Hittite, or Assyrian.

As we started off I asked where he was going. He merely pointed ahead and said, "Work." Every subsequent gambit fell flat and echoless, including (I assumed he was a Latino man) my tentative pidgin Spanish. But he accepted a drink of water from my jug, and nodded. There was a faint odor of licorice.

We were passing through the shapely shortgrass country. The man chose to gaze out the side window in silence, though the landscape didn't seem to engage him nor the open spaces to draw his focus in the least. It appeared to be a blend of shyness and preference, hands formally folded. Fine with me. Ten minutes into the trip I had given up on talking of any sort. I was entertaining those idle, scattered, heat-lightning notions that build up and flash on blank midsummer days. Suddenly the young man turned to me and waved one hand and pointed urgently out the window. I stopped the car and pulled off the highway, where he opened his door and leaned out, gagging and spitting over the berm stubble. Then he wiped his mouth with a big blue kerchief, nodded his head, and I drove on.

I began to wonder about him, where he came from, whether he was seriously ill. And the farther we went in the warm silence, the more I found myself speculating on his being in an almost involuntary way. It was a rudimentary social reflex, I suppose, seeping in to fill the speech void. I thought he might be a Basque sheepherder on furlough, hesitantly wandering out from the Bighorn Mountains. But Basques were few and far between anymore, I had heard. They had been gradually replaced by Peruvian shepherds. Well, then—he might be an itinerant Inca herder, seeing a bit of North America.

We turned south and gradually entered a more agricultural landscape: mammoth grain operations with fleets of enormous trucks and combines red-hot in the sun, miles-long feedlots with black and brown cattle in the mud. But the man seemed to find little of interest in any of it. Even the stench of the feedlots didn't faze him. He signaled to me again on a long straightaway and I pulled over to let him vomit out the door in a patch of dusty white poppies.

As we drove on, my reflexive speculation intensified of its own accord. He might be North African, or Caspian. An Anatolian gypsy. He might be pursuing a lost love around the West with a pan pipe in his blanket roll. If he could only just once get within hearing range of her—a few notes would fix it all! Or perhaps a sad young fourth-generation organ grinder whose monkey.... Things were getting out of hand in a hurry.

I stopped once more, twenty or thirty minutes later, at a pull-off overlooking a vast stretch of the North Platte river, and the man gagged again while I gazed out over the hot hazy valley. Aristotle, the Macedonian, reported that hyenas lured dogs to their death after dark by imitating the sound of a man puking. As we dropped down toward the city of Scott's Bluff the boy grew restless, squirming in his seat and glancing sidelong at me. "Do you need a doctor? *Un medico?*" A quick shake of the head.

At the first stoplight on the far north edge of town, cattycorner from that Chinese restaurant, he waved his hand and reached for his gear. He needed air; he was on to me. He took a cherry lifesaver, thanked me softly in noncommittal English and hopped from the car.

An Oklahoma Story

Shell watched the two women coming along the concourse toward him. Two similar, well dressed, snowy-haired ladies strolling arm-in-arm among the passenger waiting areas. He had seen them go by on the other side of the concourse some minutes before, exuding leisurely pleasure and real pearls; then he had returned to the window to watch the jets touch down. They were pretty women, gentle and powdered. They surveyed the waiting passengers and stopped for a moment at each and every infant or young child, stopped and gazed at them with loving smiles and appreciative eyes—*Isn't she lovely! Look at the pretty dress! Isn't he a doll*—then moving graciously on to the next one like connoisseurs through a rose garden.

Shell was at the age when for the first time he had to pause and think some days just who in his personal world was dead and who wasn't: A tallying he found both humbling and shabby. But that's what he was doing, vaguely, when he turned back toward the airport window and saw Tom E. Barlor idling there, slapping his thigh with a rolled-up *Oklahoma City News.*

"Son of a gun—hello, Shell."

"Hello, Tom E. Where are you off to?"

"I'm going to Dallas. Business. Yourself?"

"I'm going home."

That's right, still in Chicago. Just down overnight to see Uncle Dale. Not very good. He's the last of them, isn't he. He's the last of them. How are your folks. They're alright. You knew Laura Kasich died. Laura Kasich. No, when was this. Year and a half ago. I never heard. Sweet Jesus. The less I know the better, that's what I say nowadays. I wouldn't be worth a damn on a quiz show anymore. That's my plane, I'd better get on it.

"I thought you were going to Chicago."

"I change in K.C."

He had a full hour to kill in Kansas City. He went to a bar and drank a slow Scotch and looked out at the cloudy Missouri valley sky. Flocks of starlings were wheeling around the runways. Dale had asked him to smuggle a pint of Old Crow into the hospital, waited three seconds, then pretended he was joking.

An announcement came from the speaker by the television. There was a radar problem in the airport and all flights were on hold until further notice. Shell had another drink and walked over to an information counter.

"We're jammed up tight. The airport is closed until things clear up. I'm sorry."

A woman in a coyote coat was asking what the problem was.

"The problem," said the official, "is ducks, a few million ducks. They're flying south for the winter and it seems like they're all going at once this time. Our radar is completely scrambled."

"How long will it be?"

"Nobody knows, ma'am. It's wall to wall ducks. Omaha and Des Moines are shut down too."

Shell turned and walked to the window and looked up at the white November sky. He gradually realized that his body had gooseflesh moving on it and his face held an unfamiliar smile. Who in this tail end of a century would believe it? Ducks so thick they shut an airport down. Shut the Mississippi flyway down. Break the circuit even for an hour. Even for five minutes. It was like an uprising, a rebellious Mahatma Gandhi action from the least expected quarter. Ducks. Good old-fashioned ducks. Mallards, pintails, gadwalls. Canvasbacks and shovelers, rising up. Rising like a great autonomous wind.

He hurried back to the bar and ordered another drink. He told the bartender the news—*Ducks.* The man chortled. "Duck soup." Shell walked back to the window and looked at the clouds. Snow geese and specklebellies. Bluebills and ringnecks. Mergansers, goosanders. All the gray-sky cold-wind duck words. Waves of duck words shutting down the robot words and the bodiless flick-beep words screaming like bees in a jar. Even for five minutes.

He drank another whiskey and went to the men's room. He turned to the man at the next urinal, his face yellow-green under the pissoir light, and said it once more. *Ducks.*

Then he was tired. He found a seat near his jetgate and leaned back with one elbow resting on his flight bag. The Scotch was starting to thicken. He'd better get something to eat pretty soon.

He closed his eyes and dozed a little. "Twenty-nine times." One of the ridiculous catchphrases from high school that Tom E., in particular, had used unto death for six months or so. "Have you seen Eddie?" "Twenty-nine times." "Are you going to the dance?" "Twenty-nine times." From Twenty-nine Palms, California, maybe, who knows: Chimpanzee residue from some kid's family vacation to the coast. Twenty-nine palm readers. Twenty-nine mergansers overhead.

He wasn't really asleep. He heard people talking around him, so he wasn't really dreaming. But a small memory circled once and rose gently like a brightly striped fish to the top of the tank. He was driving truck, thirty years ago, part time while he went to school. He had a big load of yellow onions. Each time he stopped at a red light the aroma caught up, surged up around the cab. But on the straightaways he settled back and thought of the long, pretty, Afghan-hound face of Laura Kasich.

Shortly after he cleared the Washita River he pulled off to have lunch. He parked the truck along the road and walked over to a picnic table under half-leaved October trees with hives of mistletoe in their branches. This was the red dirt country. Shell had a ham sandwich and a piece of cake in his lunchbox.

The table was set just above a small stream, a muddy-banked turtle run choked with freckling brush and a dozen kinds of eager saplings. Shell looked at it while he unwrapped the waxed paper from his sandwich, and looked off to his right at the cotton field beyond the road, the cloud-white bolls against the deep mahogany-red soil. A wonder the cotton itself didn't turn out red. As his eye wandered he noticed an old man standing across the creek, standing straight and tall in an opening in the trees. The man had lifted his hand to shoo a fly or Shell never would have picked him out against the speckle of the various leaves. The man seemed to be watching Shell but it was too far to say for sure.

Shell ate his sandwich and wadded up the paper, then turned sideways at the table and ate the cake looking at the cotton field. Someone was walking slowly down the highway back toward the last town. When Shell turned to the creek he saw the old man was still there in the same place. Shell was closing up his lunchbox when the old man hollered, a soft whooo or whoa-o of a call, almost like a dove, with something guileless and importunate in it. The old man waved his hand as if he wanted to talk.

Shell watched him take a hesitant step in his direction, then wiped his hands on his pants and went down the red bank to the stream. He found a narrow place to jump across and climbed up the other side. The old man was waiting for him in the middle of the clearing. Shell saw now he was a one-armed man wearing giant overalls; he had a long-handled spade leaning in his hand.

"Might I ask you to help me a short while?"

The man's face was a face beyond, a face with no look at all on it. Shell followed him into a narrow neck of oak woods and out the other side where a pasture opened. The old man stopped beside a little hole at the edge of the field and turned around. There was a thin woman sitting on a log to one side.

"I can't do very well with just the one arm."

Shell looked over at the woman and a small thing wrapped in a blanket on the ground. The woman stared off through the trees. She had a wooden bowl of something or other balanced on her lap.

Shell looked at the man, the pinned-up sleeve, then pulled out his pocket watch.

"I can't go any six feet. I'm running a load of onions."

"We don't need six feet."

Shell took the shovel and started to dig. He stopped after a few minutes and took his jacket off and hung it on a branch, then dug some more. He followed the shape of the hole the old man had started. Nobody said anything while he worked.

After a quarter hour he thought the hole was alright, and the man nodded. Shell leaned the shovel against a tree and reached for his jacket, then stopped.

"You want me to fill 'er in for you?"

The old man made a show of considerate hurrying. He went for the small bundle in the blanket and carried it carefully over to the hole. Shell walked out into the scrubby pasture field a little way and wiped the perspiration off his head and rubbed the shovel spots on his hands. Blue jays were crying in the oaks. Then he went back and took the spade and filled in the hole while the old man stood beside him and the woman sat motionless on the log. When he was finished he handed the shovel to the man and then the woman got up and walked over to the grave. She threw handfuls of golden chinaberries from the bowl onto the fresh dirt, tossed them casually, as if she were feeding chickens.

Shell walked back to the creek and hopped across it and up the bank to the table. He was thankful the old man had let him eat before calling him over. He picked up his lunchbox and jug of water and walked toward the truck.

There was a gray-haired woman with her hairpins lost and gone standing in the pull-off beside an old Studebaker with its hood raised. Shell opened the truck door and turned back with one foot on the step-up.

"I'm sorry, ma'am. I'm done for the day."

Bunker With Pines

JT was hunting turkeys and I was along for the ride, for the Tongue River hills and an hour or two of his gruff wandering talk in vestigial Arkansas cadence, excitable and truth-careless as a child's, offhand as a belly rumble.

It was less hunting than it was shooting, or reaping; all the work, if you could call it that, the two-legged figuring, had been done well ahead of time. JT owned a marble-eyed blue heeler. He threw the dog in the back of his pickup truck and we drove away from his trailer home with his twelve-gauge shotgun leaning between us, across the river and up into the piney hills. He turned off down a lumber road along the ridge and settled in at five miles an hour.

Now he was hunting. When the dog smelled turkeys near at hand she began to jump and whine and scratch at the back of the cab and JT stopped the truck. The dog dashed off into the woods and rushed the flock, which flew routinely up into the trees to avoid the yapping nuisance, and JT shot one, often from the edge of the road, his heavy white body crouched bowlegged to take aim, hardly breaking the stride of the story he was twirling at the time.

When we crossed a narrow valley-crease in the hills, I noticed a poorly homestead set back off the road, a rough sort of place with a bristly, barricaded look to it: small dread-faced windows and heavy fences around a defoliated yard with no soft edges. "That's a funny outfit there," JT said. And he told me about them as he dropped into low gear for the rutted grade.

Like many great schisms, it began over a piece of rotten meat.

The family had moved up to Montana from Denver several years before. The man's name was Appadurai, he was of Indian—East Indian—descent. His family had operated a small print shop for years in Denver, a sooty storefront on lower Broadway among the wig wholesalers and cut-rate spaghetti parlors and tattoo salons. They printed every sort of petty odd job from wedding announcements to chop suey menus, but their specialty had gradually become, since the 1960s, bumper stickers for automobiles.

Appadurai and his cousin ran the place, with an ever-shifting mix of distant relatives standing by. They cranked out bumper stickers covering the political gamut from Mao to Hitler, every strain of bigotry and erotic preference, every childish peeve and righteous cause; they touted sports teams, Paraguayan ancestry, and hatred of the state of Texas. They all rolled off the same press and went bundled out the same back door into the same low-slung station wagon. Appadurai stickers caused a man to be shot at the wheel (minor flesh wound) in Missouri and a poor old woman (a devout pantheist) to be rammed viciously from behind at a stoplight in Roswell, New Mexico. Appadurai thought them up himself for the most part, rising early in the morning to daydream with his eyes half-closed and scan the newspapers for volatile issues of the day.

Appadurai married a Cheyenne woman he met at a South Denver bingo game. They lived quietly by television light in a small half-house a few blocks from the shop with their baby boy and a tank of nervous guppies. Appadurai's cousin and workmate lived alone not far away. The cousin was a murky, locked-in man, a notorious miser built like an ichneumon fly, with muddy red-flecked half-moons under his eyes. He smoked contemplatively all day and much of the night and once a month fished alone in the lake at Washington Park, straight-faced as a heron, until he had enough in his plastic pail to make a grapefruit-colored curry.

One Sunday afternoon the cousin was sitting with the family at the Appadurai house. A popular uncle and three other cousins were there, too, and a woman friend with her hair rolled, long known to them all. They had eaten earlier in the day and were gathered in the kitchen chatting and smoking. The toddler boy stood in the midst embracing a table leg.

Appadurai was after something in the refrigerator, leaning and reaching, and discovered a dish of food wrapped in foil. Peeking cautiously under the wrapping—"Oof, these chicken livers are a year old!"

He moved toward the garbage basket in the corner, but the cousin, with a quick and waltzlike step, intercepted.

"Let me see, I might take them home with me for supper."

Appadurai protested, laughing, waving a hand. The livers were no good, they had been in the refrigerator for weeks.

"Just let me see them, maybe they are alright."

"They are green as grass. They smell bad. They are too old."

By now the rest of the family attended. The cousin was trying to reach past Appadurai to take the dish. Appadurai was holding it beyond his reach, still laughing a raspy defensive laugh.

"Just let me smell them. I tell you they are probably alright."

Now all the family was chuckling nervously. The cousin flushed and looked back at them as if he'd forgotten they were there. Appadurai took advantage and lunged to the garbage basket and flung the livers away and closed the lid and sat on it. He was perspiring across the brow. The cousin straightened and looked at him for a brief moment with a bitter expression of formally registered insult and dismay.

The favorite uncle raised a waggish eyebrow, unfolded his legs, and said from across the room, "You must be starving, nephew. I will buy you something for supper."

Three years passed. The print shop prospered. Appadurai decided to have his son's horoscope made in honor of the child's sixth birthday. It was by tradition a ceremonious affair. The Coming of Boyhood. The Winging of the Bird. Appadurai's cousin was the only person he knew who was qualified to prepare such a thing. After closing the shop one night, Appadurai approached him, petitioned him in a grand manner to take on the job. They stood before a hubcap clearing house. A full horoscope was complicated, studious work. The cousin would charge a hundred dollars. Appadurai nodded thoughtfully. The deal was struck.

Six weeks after, on a damp March evening, the cousin came into the back room of the shop where Appadurai was sorting and loading a box of bumper stickers ("Make Mine Pomeranian," bound for southern California). The cousin waited quietly until Appadurai taped the box. Then he handed him a large brown envelope, took two fifty dollar bills in return, and left the building. His viscera tingled and his palms were damp. He was so pleased with himself that he stopped for a cup of coffee and a scoop of ice cream before walking home.

No one knows what exactly the horoscope promised the boy, but it was bad enough that Appadurai closed the shop for three days and drew the curtains tight at home. By the second evening his normally even-keeled wife had contracted his shuddering terror and they sat on the couch with the boy between them, whispering over the details and shaking their heads. Two days later they packed up, took what money they had in the bank, and left town in the early dawn.

In Montana they settled in the little Indian house on land belonging to the wife's family. They doubled the fences and halved the windows, cut back the plum brush from the yard and strengthened the locks. They live for the most part on the Cheyenne woman's government checks. They use her family name now: Pin Cherry, Cherry for short. Rarely go out of the house.

Just after noon we came back that road, came bumping down the hill with five turkeys in the back and the dog sound asleep among them. When we passed the house there was a tall man standing below an ash tree near the fence. He had a fat prairie dog on a harness-leash and turned to watch as our truck went by. From a leafy limb above his shoulder a set of barefooted legs dangled in yellow pajama pantaloons.

"That's Appadurai."

"Who's up in the tree?"

"That must be Breece, the boy."

Faery Tale for a Large Child

That November morning the Flicker River was running on schedule and by 8 o'clock the sun was bright through gauzy clouds. The northern horizon line held stolid blackbottomed cloud banks, but the late autumn palomino of the prairie was for the moment light and sun-brightened. Horses stood happy in the bluestem swales.

By noon the northwest skyline was brooding dark, but the sun still shone overhead. The white buttes off to the north stood out sharply, almost glaring against the wintry clouds. A man was walking around the town of Flicker in search of company. He was a thin, stooped man about fifty, wearing overalls and a flannel shirt; a good-natured man with a small Bible in his pants pocket, and he was looking for company.

He walked along Railroad Street paralleling the tracks. There was a small public park there, but no one was in it right then, and no one was sitting under the elm trees farther along, or on the weedy loading dock of the superannuated grain mill. And there was nobody Indian at the counter of the little diner when he peered in the window.

But when he turned the corner onto Main Street he saw his pal Ed coming down the block. Ed had a sack of beer under his arm and the two men went back to the little park and sat at the picnic table there and sipped at their beers. Ed wore a cap that said "Houghton Sulky." They watched a crew in the railyard put together a freight train, coupling and switching. It was like a rodeo event. The completed train geared up and ground out toward the east. The two men waved at the engineer as it passed and when it was gone they could see the blackening clouds hanging heavy in the north.

When the beer was finished they cached the empty cans under a bush where they could find them later and sell them across town. Then they walked down the main thoroughfare and went into a saloon called the Horseshoe.

"Looks like snow."

They walked around the bar to the back room. There was a woman they knew in one of the booths and they sat with her and ordered beers. The woman was a quiet one; she had her winter coat on, a coniferous tweed. The three of them watched some boys shooting pool on the far side of the room.

In a while another woman came into the bar by herself and found the threesome in the back. She was a younger, pretty-in-a-way woman who used to live in Rapid City. Pretty even though she kept one eye closed all the time as though there were a cinder in it. The foursome ordered more beer and a plate of french fries with cheese melted on them.

The man with the little Bible in his overalls was named Moses. He pulled the Bible out to get a twenty-dollar bill from it. The young woman teased him about being a preacher, a preacher named Moses. He leaned back and read them a line from Romans, chapter 14: "Let not her who does not eat judge him who eats." And everyone laughed.

Then a young man joined them. He was a distant relative of the woman in the tweed coat. He was an artist, a sculptor and painter. Born and raised in a small reservation town where many of the boys were slender and womanly, a town known for them in fact, the well-dressed boys with fashionably coifed shining hair strolling about with often an adoring entourage of young children in their wake, he was slender and womanly in both bearing and speech. His sleek black hair hung in a ponytail to his waist. Because he liked nice clothing and wore fancy off-color shoes the people called him "Dago." He painted, among the tipi reveries and white buffalo scenes, portraits of local cowboys with their sleeves rolled up on shapely arms, relaxed on a pinto pony or lolling against a corral fence.

In half an hour they decided to drive over to Rushton. Dago had a car. The fivesome got in and he drove them slowly around town. They were laughing and joking and looking for any friends they might find on the streets. They checked the alleyways and sunny corners. They bought gasoline and beer and cigarettes and drove out the east side of town.

It was thirty miles to Rushton. The sun was still out, thin but casting shadows. The prairie by now was mouse-colored, dog-colored, with nothing of brightness on it but the soapweed. The clouds in the north were jet black.

Rushton was a mean town, with meanness in its wind and in its water, but they hoped to see some people there. They felt like having a party while the sun held out. They drove slowly down the main street, past the saloons and ranchware stores. The woman in the tweed coat saw a boy she knew on the corner and they stopped and talked. He was a cousin of her half sister; he wore a Chicago Bulls shirt. They brought him into the car and drove to a public park on the edge of town and the six of them got out and sat at the table and drank beer. Another old man hobbled up to talk for a minute, then walked on.

"Looks like snow."

They stopped talking to watch a freight train go through. Loaded high with Wyoming coal. They all waved at the engine crew. The boy in the Bulls shirt turned on a pocket radio. The young woman was teasing Moses about his name again. He cleared his throat and read them a verse from Zechariah. "So they answered the Angel of the Lord, who stood among the myrtle trees, and said, 'We have walked to and fro throughout the earth, and behold, all the earth is resting quietly.'"

Eventually they decided to drive back to Flicker. It was a better town. They knew more people over there. They stashed their empty cans under a bush and went back to the navy Plymouth Duster. Moses walked tall and carefully now. They stopped for more beer at a gas station.

The day had finally changed, caught up. The clouds in the north had moved overhead almost suddenly, almost with a lunge. The air was colder. All color had bled from the day save a pencil-thin line of bright white on the very western skyline.

They drove west through the village of Rushton. Just beyond the city limits where the road got dark they saw a man in a black coat walking along the highway with his collar up against the wind.

"Looks like Joe."

They backed up and waited for the man to come on. He knew everyone in the car. He got in the backseat and the old Plymouth sagged. Moses and Ed and the woman in the winter coat were back there with him. The painter, the young woman, and the boy in the

Bulls shirt were up front. A sevensome. The heater had the car warm and smelling like winter.

It was almost dark, earlier than usual. The young man in the Bulls shirt was starting to like the young woman beside him. She was pretty even with the one eye closed. She knew what was what, and no Monkey Business. He thought about her and felt her shoulder against him as he looked out the window.

The wind picked up from the north. The tall grass along the road began to lean and shimmy and the old oriole nests began to rock on their bare branches. Dago at the wheel was beginning to think about the boy in the Bulls shirt. He was a nice kid with nice hands and fingers and eyes.

A few minutes later the snow came jabbing, light but insistent, angling in low from the north. The dirt mounds of the prairie dog towns were the first things to hold white in the very tag end of twilight. A cigarette lighter flared in the backseat. Someone said "Bingo." Someone else said "Bango." The Plymouth went off through a fence and over a hill and rolled across a dried-up gully with oil cans and dirty diapers in it. And the rivers pulled their willows close overhead for the night.

Talk Across Water

Just after sundown three boys with pellet guns climbed the rickety fire escape on a gutted old school building in Montana. It was a simple case of groundling-airborne grudge: Nothing else to do that provocative time of day unless you were a singer of Sky chanteys but go up there to the ratty flat roof and smoke and fire spitefully at the laggard last of the nighthawks veering through the pastel evening overhead and out of reach.

It was late October, clear and mild. Every scratch and whisper carried like talk across water. At one end of the little town a group of Indian kids were back again at the poor Dunkard's bedroom window, crouched in the fresh darkness to hear the man carry on. The poor Dunkard, a man of forty with a face like a scrubbed shoat and a touch of the walleye and a shock of red medieval hair, after thirty years of inadvertent near-saintly religious life during which he lived with his mother and existed, thrived, fattened even, on a serene two-tone vocabulary of a dozen German phrases repeated over and over as needed—*Gottes Wille; Gott denkt; mehr Butter; Gott weiss, jawohl*—after thirty years of it he had been stricken two weeks earlier with the Babbling Disease and except for a brief tight-lipped flurry of household chores in the early morning he lay all his waking hours on a turn-of-the-twentieth-century divan or stretched on his narrow bed unleashing a torrent of German-English blend even his mother could not grasp in full or slow. And the neighboring kids crept in below his window like cats and listened with an honest awe to his rapid-fire mix of tongues and tones and hymns rendered barnyard risqué, while his mother rocked resignedly at his side through nightfall awaiting the curtain of sleep.

Far to the east that very hour, a boy with a book was committing to memory the various plumages of the eastern nighthawk, the fluid, almost lunar progression from "tilleul" through "Quaker drab" and "fuscous" to "vinaceous-buff," and envisioning the legendary pure albino specimen seen one summer at Lynchburg, Virginia, streaking, talked about all up and down the coast, through their pastel 1886 sky; and a man was bent at desk stroking one earlobe, writing, "Suppose, of all the overlooked and latent Power-Whorls of this world, that Melancholy, born of long experience, distilled from generations of the complex relations we live within, proved in the end to be the most transformative and incendiary of them all."

And early next morning a middle-aged woman drank an extra cup of coffee and ate an extra donut for her day off and drove from one side of the little town to the outskirts of the other to pick up her elderly aunt. "It's Halloween," she said when the old woman was settled in the car.

"Then we had better hurry up and get home before dark." The aunt was a perky little woman whose eyes were mostly gone. You wouldn't know it to see her drink a cup of Nescafé, but her great-great-great-grandmother was among those women crushed by the fickle riverbank while they were digging paint clay one afternoon 200 years before. The people named that stream after them, that temperamental tributary of the Powder where lark sparrows sing—River Where the Cliff Caved in on the Women— but even so, only a dozen souls on earth knew that old name now.

They drove from town and up into the grassy red and yellow hills. "It's a pretty day," the younger woman said. The aunt cupped both her hands around her one decent eye and looked attentively out the window. "Yes it is," she finally agreed. "It's like a summer day."

"Gee, we were busy at the hospital yesterday," the niece was telling. "They had a big fight over at the river. A whole lot of fishermen got in a fight and beat each other up. They brought six or seven of them in to get fixed up."

"Which river?"

"Over there on the Bighorn."

"What were they fighting about anyhow?"

"All those boats get out there in the river and they run into each other or get too close and get tangled up in the lines. Then they get mad and start yelling and then they start swinging the oars and everything. Some of them were cut up pretty bad, too."

"I never did like fish anyway. Not enough to fight about it."

"I'll take my tuna casserole and leave the rest."

"I never did like tuna fish either."

They were driving up a narrow dirt road by now. At the crest of the hill was a small cemetery. They got out and walked through the creaky gate and the old woman paused with her hand above her eyes and gazed around the plot familiarly, as if she had entered a room she hadn't visited for a good while. "Watch out for rattlesnakes." Then she hobbled over to the family stones and rummaged in her purse, set a package of cigarettes below each one and whacked once or twice with her cane at the weeds behind them.

The young woman took her arm and they strolled among the graves, reading the names, saying them aloud as if to freshen them, keep them on the air and on the continent itself.

"Billy Far," the niece read, and the old woman nodded as she did each time they came.

"Billy Far," she answered. "He was a good boy. Then his wife ran away with that soldier. First thing Billy did was start up a band. They played all around here, on the reservation and off. Played those real sad songs that make you thirsty. Beer-drinking songs. He had that band for a year. Everyone thought he was over his wife leaving. Thought all those songs had got him over it. So he gave up the band all of a sudden. But then he started drinking real bad. He got drunk one night so bad he walked out in front of a train. Over by Hardin."

She told the niece once again about the Shirts, their two stones set a few feet apart with a chokecherry sprout taking hold between them. They had been married ten or fifteen years when Iris, Mrs. Shirt, told Delwin he had to get out. No reason given. Delwin moved out into an old garage a few rods down the hill and lived there the rest of his long life. Iris set up the gravestones for them, but put a little extra distance between them. Delwin never did know why she kicked him out.

"And this fellow—Willis Wagon—He lived over around Cat Creek. He was a holy man, I guess they call it. Knew all about the ceremonies. Tobacco Society and all those things. He did everything real slow, like the holy men are supposed to. Always moved real slow and careful. He used to walk out to the mailbox by the road and it would take him an hour to get back. His wife would start to worry about him, go looking out all the windows.

"Kind of funny—his boy was a stock car racer."

A starling in the cemetery's single tree was luxuriating in the sun, squawking and whistling, mimicking a killdeer, then a nighthawk, a May meadowlark, a peacock yowl he had picked up over in Billings. The women walked hand-in-hand back to the car.

"Maybe we should stop at the Corners and get something to eat."

They parked at the rural roadhouse and walked across the parking lot. All the hackberry trees had dropped their curled-up leaves several days before and each step made a crunch and a crackle. They took a table near the door and ordered hamburgers. The waitress and the man behind the bar wore Halloween get-ups. The girl was dressed as a sort of ranch-hand vampire and the man wore a mask of Fidel Castro with an arrow piercing his skull, left to right.

The women were finishing their coffee when another Halloweener entered the place. He came shuffling through the door and turned heavily to the customers, staring dumbly through a pustuled and warted neo-Neanderthal mask with wild monkey hair flying from it. He wore a greasy long bathrobe with burrs and chicken feathers on it, hanging open to reveal a huge lifelike phallus the size of a ballbat, swaying bruised and scar-mottled and heavily veined to the man's calves. The patrons at the bar greeted him with a Ha and a Ho. He finally began to shuffle into the place, slow and humpbacked, pausing at each table to gape at the diners.

The two women peeked at him sideways when he stood beside them breathing hoarsely through his mouth. The niece giggled into her napkin. The old one finally set down her coffee and cupped her hands at her decent eye and looked again. She began to chuckle and shake her head, and the man lurched on toward the bar.

"You can see better than you let on, Auntie," the niece said when they were out in the parking lot.

"Oh my. He's going to put someone's eye out with that thing. Reminds me of my first boyfriend. It was always Halloween with him around."

Off to the east a full day's drive, a girl on a late-afternoon sofa was reading and stroking a Siamese cat: "Be assured the slightest fragment of bird song is not uttered in vain. During periods of sexual calm, it is the tireless rehearsal for the great concerts of love."

The women drove back through the summer-like day. The old one cupped her hands once to see if anyone was home at a certain sumac-red house on a hill. As they walked up to the aunt's front door the niece told her, "Now lock your doors and stay inside tonight. Close your curtains tight. Tomorrow is All Saints' Day. It will be safe to come out then."

"I'll be alright. No goblins want to fool with me—except maybe some old skeleton. I'm going to be busy anyway. I'll be busy praying for that Halloween man's wife."

Echofield

The old woman had a job cooking all summer at the Catholic boarding school. Every workday her husband drove her halfway across the reservation and dropped her, in her hair net, at the kitchen door at 8 o'clock sharp. Then he drove a short ways up the dirt road climbing the hill behind the brick buildings and parked his car in the shade of a grove of trees. He waited there all day until 3 o'clock when his wife got off work. He listened to several different stations on the radio. He took short walks along the hillside and occasionally climbed up to look over the top of the hill. He swatted flies. Sometimes he picked a hatful of chokecherries or black currants. He took long, away-from-home naps with his cap down over his eyes. Every day at 12:30 his wife brought a plate from the cafeteria up the hill and they ate together and talked in the front seat of the car.

One warm day she brought a big platter of meat loaf and mashed potatoes and after she went back down the hill the man decided he had eaten so much he had better get in the backseat and stretch out for a real nap. He even took off his shoes. And pretty soon the kingbirds had him dreaming.

He dreamed a long, out-of-the-ordinary dream that moved around from place to place. There was a white man and his white wife, people the old man didn't recognize. The man had married this girl—she was a ranch girl—and taken her off to a big city where he worked. It might have been Omaha. The girl got tired of it after a while and the husband loved her so much that he took her back to the country and built them a nice ranch house somewhere around Kaycee, Wyoming. They had air conditioning and two or three big horse trailers and a swimming pool. They were all settled in and comfortable, you could see that in the dream.

The woman was crazy about paint horses. She was soon in charge of a pretty herd. She spent long days with them, caring for them and brushing their manes and tails. Her husband was proud of his wife's hard work with the paints. He told his friends she paid more attention to the horses than she did to himself.

One morning the man needed to talk to his wife about some important business. He knew where to find her. He drove his pickup down the valley and out along a wooded ridge overlooking the range where the painted horses were grazing. He stopped at the edge of the pines and picked up his binoculars to scan the herd and locate his wife. He spotted her right away on one edge of the meadow. She was standing with the big paint stallion, a wildish horse with pale blue milky eyes. She had her arms around his neck and was hugging him and stroking his shoulders. Some of the mares were standing around them, watching. The husband was watching too, through his binoculars. When the dream turned around and showed him he had a terrible look on his face. The woman's clothing was folded in a neat pile to one side and the stallion was beginning to neigh and shuffle with his tail in the air.

The old dreamer jerked awake in the backseat of his car. He got up on one elbow and scratched his head roughly. The dream made him uncomfortable. He knew where it came from; it came straight from an old story the old people used to tell about the old days—a woman falling in love with a pretty red-speckled horse. It was a story lots of people had heard—the jealous husband would shoot the stallion and make more trouble—but never with white people in it.

It made the old man feel annoyed. He had just wanted a little nap. Those ranch people might be people he knew after all, and that dream might be none of his business.

Maybe it was the meat loaf that got everything mixed up. He got out of the car and straightened his shirt and tucked it in his pants, then walked down to the mission faucet in his stocking feet to splash cold water over his head, three or four times.

One Summer by the River

Each evening for fifteen years Henry Swainson has packed his redwood easel and a holster of paints and hobbled down the half-mile path from his home to the east bank of the Missouri River, smiling and licking his lips. He has painted the Dakota landscape for more than fifty years; stretched oils, hand-size acrylics, and quick charcoal cartoons lean three and four deep along his humble studio walls. Canyons, badlands, ghostly buffalo herds plodding the coulees.... But at sunrise on his eightieth birthday he decided in a flood of liberating clarity to give up all subjects but one: sunset over the big, bulling river.

It might sound at first like an old man's fatuous surrender. But Henry is a gifted tonalist, neither a dabbler nor a dupe, and his decision was a masterful sharpening of focus and a conservation of energy worthy of a desert mammal. He loves awakening each day to find the Missouri still there, dependable as a dog. He loves its bulldozer sureness, its interchangeable gulls and random flotsam, and most of all the colors it begs from the Dakota sky. And every evening finds him there, accordingly, painting from a fertile trance where adoration flirts with and bleeds into dotage, singing aloud to himself on the breezy shore—"I Remember You" or "The Moon was Shining Bright Upon the Wabash."

That particular summer he was searching almost daily for an elusive shade of blue that he had never noticed before, a blue that visited the western sky for a brief vesperal moment just above the bands of apricot and flame. Henry mixed and matched and remixed and made notes on the hue as one might make notes on an exceptional wine. It was neither periwinkle nor Kelly nor kingfisher blue. It had morning glory in it, but also flax and jay and a subconscious pulse of winter-heron that bordered on lapis. All summer he worked at it. And he would find it eventually, this season or next, strike it one evening while singing "Just One of Those Things." He already had a name for it: "True Old Mandan Blue."

*****

That was the summer the young people in the little Indian town began to dress like the old. It came on gradually, like weather or blossom. Took root on an afternoon much like this one, maybe, somewhere in the makeshift village set on a hillside on the west bank of the Missouri, the gulls sailing. The young people—sixteen-, eighteen-year-olds—began watching the old. On one corner a boy stood studying the two old men walking carefully down the street. Studied the hitch of their gait, the hang of their worn clothing. At the edge of town, where you could look straight down and see the river below, a dawdling brother and sister watched a rheumatic old man labor across a lawn to examine a chokecherry bush; he moved with a lurch, then a tiptoe. Lurch, then tiptoe.

Blocks away, a group of girls began to notice the old women in their kerchiefs and heavy sand-colored stockings. They all turned their heads at once and began to notice, biting casually at their fingernails or idly stretching a strand of hair. And, on a day like that, without collusion or program or even worded thought, the thing was set in motion.

*****

It was also the summer they found the dead German man along the river ten miles north of town. A tourist-photographer from Stuttgart, he had, it seemed, been murdered in the night and his head cut off and presumably thrown into the Missouri. An old woman had discovered the corpse early the following morning.

The police chief in the little town took the report and drove up to the scene of the crime with a deputy. They stopped first at the small house of a man named Robert Onions. The house was a hundred yards or so from where the body had been found. Onions came out to meet them. He was a man nearing seventy years, tall and lean, of good nerve and bountiful inner life, who spent a great deal of time nowadays sitting by the river. He had noticed nothing out of the ordinary the night before. Maybe a car door or two slamming at some point, but that was not unusual. The place they found the headless man was a small parking area at a crumbling one-time boat ramp. People used it all the time for swimming, drinking, propagating the species.

"Beatrice. She can tell you about it."

Beatrice Voice, an eighty-three-year-old utterly blind Hunkpapa woman, had discovered the body. She lived in an old house with seared elm trees just upriver from Onions, fifty yards beyond the boat ramp. She was sitting on her porch beside a headstrong trumpet vine when the police drove up.

"God bless you boys. I've been blind since I was forty years old. I was working at the trading post in Mobridge and that cleaning lye splashed in my face and I went blind three days later. I only remember a few colors. But I hear pretty good. Better than most. I can hear a baby cry on the other side of the river on a clear night.

"Last night I woke up and heard some loud music. It must be a car radio. Then I heard people yelling. It sounded like some kind of a fight started. Banging around, hollering. Then it got real quiet for a while. Then I heard someone start to chopping and hacking away and I knew right away they were cutting through bone. I could tell by the sound of it. Like butchering a beef. I know that sound my whole life. Then I heard a kind of a splash, a kind of kerplunk like a watermelon, then the car drove off. Sounded like an old car, not running real good. Ping-ping-ping Chang! Ping-ping-ping Chang! That's how it ran.

"When it got daylight I walked over there right away and poked around with my cane. Rotgut bottles all over the place. And there was that body over next to the bullberry bushes. I could feel it with my cane and I could smell the blood. I know that smell all my life. That's when I sent for my granddaughter and had her call you up right away. God bless you boys! My name is Beatrice Voice."

*****

That week the young people began showing up in town dressed like old people. Just a few at first, Delano and his sister Eliza, and

88

one or two of their friends. They walked down the street, went to the store and the post office, the usual daily things. The boys wore baggy secondhand trousers held up with suspenders over faded white shirts. Old dusty clodhopper shoes, or outmoded narrow dress shoes dating from the 1930s. The girls wore pale, thin print dresses with shawls over them, and black, lace-up Model-T shoes.

The Marine Corps recruiter from Aberdeen was one of the first to notice. He was in town on his quarterly rounds, sizing up the Indian boys as they played basketball or baseball or shot fish with .22 rifles from the creek bridges, looked them over good with a toothpick flexing in his teeth. Every year he found one or two of the right heft and stature and talked to them for a long time on each of his visits, took them off to one side and talked to them in a low avuncular salesman voice about becoming a U.S. Marine and, if they timed it right, being able to wear the fresh-pressed uniform down the aisle at high school graduation. When he saw the first of the young people dressed like the old he looked over at the café waitress and rolled his hazel eyes: "If you say so!"

A few days later there were more. They showed up in small groups at any time of day. Some had driven matter-of-factly to Bismarck to shop in the thrift stores. They had soft old Stetsons and well-worn sportcoats, old bolo ties and neckerchiefs and antiquated sunglasses. Girls came down the street under parasols three times their own age.

It was no simple prank. It was an odd, almost atmospheric mimicry both harsh and thoughtful. A mime that came on without premeditation, like flowers on a bush. If you asked them, the young people might have said that Delano and his sister were probably the source of the idea; from them it spread quietly but surely, without smirk or smile or even consultation. It was an instinctive generational reflex the young people couldn't explain themselves, and didn't try.

And the old looked on with a cautious attention, like fox, or deer. They watched the mime gather and rise with amused intelligent eyes. The old clothing inspired a mild worldly nostalgia, as if the particular parasols and suspenders themselves were recognized after a long absence. It was an unsuspected but welcome phenomenon they appreciated and were curious about but left alone, knowing it wasn't theirs. Robert Onions watched the girls go by in calico dresses and Model-T shoes, saw Eliza in the blue dress, and said to his crony in the shade, "She makes me think of Lottie Teal."

By the middle of July it crested. On a Saturday noon the little main street was full of people, as it was most Saturdays, but now the mime was on in full flower. The west side of the street was crowded with the young in their old outfits, going about their normal Saturday business. On the east sidewalk the old walked slowly along or rested out of the sun, watching. The mirror image was in place. Some of the thoughtful elders, like Onions, knew there was a glint of parody and mockery in the mime. But not enough to matter. There was also a hint of lying calmly facedown in the yearling grass in resignation, not to see the sky and clouds go streaming by.

By now, whether they knew it or not, the young people had adopted the slightest stoops and gaits of the old, the tilt of the frail boneage. The old people noted all the details with relish. "She dresses like my aunt Carlotta used to dress." Robert Onions was looking and thinking, enjoying himself. Finally he walked slowly across the street and up to Eliza in the blue calico. He removed his Stetson and formally presented himself: Robert Onions.

"People think Onions is an Indian name, but it's not. My great grandfather was half English. Canadian. Onions is an English name. There are still people over in England named Onions."

Beatrice Voice was there, in the hardware shadows. She had a daughter with her to describe the mime. "They're trying to straighten things out," she decided. "They had better be real careful."

It went on all morning. Onions walked back across to the shaded side of the street. "They're trying to shake things up. The years and the people. They're trying to break up the logjam."

*****

The bereaved German parents were still there. They were staying at the Royal Motel in Bismarck. They refused to return to Stuttgart without their son's head; they would wait if it took all summer.

The police were milling without a clue. They had garnered no information from anyone since Beatrice Voice gave them the audio description the morning after. They assigned a pair of deputies to walk the Missouri banks each day to watch for the victim's missing part. And they stationed a capable man on the main streets of Bismarck and Mandan for a while to listen carefully for the Ping-ping-ping Chang! of the incriminated car. But mostly the police force drove daily from overlook to overlook above the river, gregariously speculating and looking off from the bluffs for inspiration.

Henry Swainson sometimes saw their car mirrors flash from his spot downstream and across the Missouri. He was painting hard this particular evening, reciting to himself a gimpy ballad he had discovered in his inner repertory and come to favor.

> Up Bunker Hill, down Okinawa—
> Boys will dream when the air grows careless.
> Through Gettysburg and Belleau Woods,
> All day they dream the Mexican Hairless.
>
> The Philippines and old Verdun—
> Her legs were long, her beauty peerless.
> Pea Ridge, Manassas, Corregidor—
> Muck and mire, they dream the Mexican Hairless.
>
> San Juan Hill and Yorktown—
> Thoughts are lean and the sunshine fearless.
> Shiloh, the Bulge, the Plains of Abe—
> All day they dream the Mexican Hairless.

He was at the same time composing in his mind a letter to the editor of a regional newspaper that had printed a dubious review of Henry's paintings—a trifling handful of them—on exhibit in a quiet bank lobby. Something about an "irresponsible palette" and a "disturbing fungoid orange."

Henry composed his reply fastidiously. He wanted to get it right in two or three sentences and be done with it. Boot the young pup and be done with it....

"My dear sir. As anyone familiar in any degree with the history of the upper Missouri River in the Dakota territory would well know, there has, for some century and a half, existed in that region a unique and unmistakable shade of orange, an orange endemic to the upper Missouri, let it be said, owing its origin to the advent of ground turmeric (the well known culinary spice) among the Mandan and Hidatsa peoples of this locale, in whose villages the Caucasian traders sold it as a potent and highly esteemed dye to be applied by native artisans to such materials as porcupine quills, feathers, or the most delicate buckskins (obtained in trade from nomadic hunters of the more westerly prairies), where its chanterelle hue was immediately at home beside the local clay-derived paints of the Knife River quarries. But, tiresome to say, given the all-too-common anomaly of a modern viewer lacking the slightest familiarity with such historical subtleties, such a proto-orange in a landscape might well pulse on unappreciated in unseeing eyes beneath prematurely raised bushy eyebrows...."

Boot the young whippersnapper and be done with it.

***

A few days later the phenomenon began to unravel. Just as the first ash leaves went golden in the coulees there was a tacit sense of *Enough* in the young people and the mime began to slow. Cicadas began to sing, a few at a time, in the dusty trees.

Some of the girls decided to visit Beatrice Voice before the thing was over. They needed, without saying so, to sit with an old woman in their antique garb and leach whatever iota of sarcasm had been in the mime from the start. It wasn't much, but it would be best to sit there for an hour and leach it beside an old woman who had strangled puppies in her day for the feast foods and thrown them on the fire to burn off the hair and butchered them for the big iron kettle.

Eliza was waiting in front of the post office for her friends. She wore the calico dress she washed out every night and held the bleached lavender parasol rolled up in her hand. But she had her own shoes on today. Onions came out of the post office and walked over to her. "You look nice in that dress." He told her about the Chickasaw Nightingale, an Indian girl named Daisy Underwood from Ardmore, Oklahoma. A beautiful voice. Studied music in all the good schools out east. Toured the whole U.S.A. This was back about 1920. She sang for Tetrazini herself. "My mother heard her on the radio down in Tulsa. Oh, she had a beautiful voice. They called her the Chickasaw Nightingale. Then she ran off and married some rich oil man."

Eliza and the girls drove north on the little highway, following the river, and down the hill to Beatrice Voice's house. She was standing in her yard with both hands on her cane, listening. "God bless you girls!" The young sat in a row along the edge of her porch in their old print dresses and talked a little and dawdled with their shoes, asked a formal question or two.

"I was born in 1902, over there west of Mud Creek. I grew up over there and then we moved over to Bluestem. That's where I got married the first time. That was 1919."

"Who was there?"

"Who was there? In 1919? I'll tell you who was there! Ice was there. Old Ice and young Ice. The Burgoyne girls were there. The Berry sisters from McLaughlin were there, and so were some of their brothers. All those Hawks were there, and some of the Teals—Lottie Teal was there. Dirt was there. Box Elder was there. Willy Nilly and the Red Birds were there.

"Everyone was there." She began waving her cane like a baton. "Fog was there. Lungs was there. Duck Legs was there, and Froglips. Throw-up was there. And old Squashballs was there, too. And Dog Droppings. Rotten Bone was there. And Ghost Pecker, junior and senior. And Flies-on-the-Arse—he was there. He was always around there somewhere."

Downstream two miles a band of boys were bathing in the Missouri. They waded in up to their hams, lathered, then lobbed the bar of soap upstream just far enough that it floated back by when it was needed. They dressed, hiked up the old suspenders and the formless pants, and drove slowly up the rough dirt road to Robert Onions's.

Onions was standing down on the riverbank. He had lived beside the Missouri his entire life. He had thrown things in and pulled things out and wondered momentarily about things coursing by too far out to reach. When he saw the boys getting out of the car and putting on their big second-hand Stetsons he hollered and walked up to greet them. After a while he said, "Let me show you what I found in the river this morning."

He returned from the house carrying a plastic toy rowboat a couple of feet long. Lashed carefully into it were fifteen or twenty human figures made from wooden clothespins. They looked like homecrafted Christmas tree ornaments, angels or choirboys robed in red and white ribbon, with simple beatific expressions drawn on their faces. They all reclined face-up in rows, braced, it seemed, to run a cataract or plunge over a fall. Onions poured out a half-cup of brownish bilge-water and showed the boat around to all the boys. Later he turned aside to Delano and said, "You look good in that hat."

*****

Several days after, Delano and Onions were walking, unbeknownst to each other, the back country breaks along Mink River, the wide quiet valley a few miles west of the Missouri. The morning was cool and the sunflowers moist to the touch. Delano was moving slowly downriver. He was alone and looking for something, some thing private, you could see that from the way he walked, some thing beneficial and sure for the finding, small enough to fit in a shirt pocket. Maybe sweetgrass or osier bark. He was coming down the valley from the west.

Onions was walking up from the east, up the valley not far from the stream, and he had the same walk, the same way of moving and gently looking, around at the ground and up at the low honey-colored bluffs lining the valley. A person sitting on the top there would see at once that he was looking for something quiet and personal, too. Maybe Black Sampson root, maybe flag root to sweeten the breath.

The old man and the young moved toward one another, each with their easy wandering zigzag. Meadowlarks flushed before them and blackbird flocks lifted scolding from the sunflower beds. And then, from far off, the men saw each other. A simple enough recognition—anyone could be walking that Mink valley one or two at a time—that instantly included the privacy of the other's mission. And the approach from that point on became a kind of ballet. Neither showed a sign of having seen the other. They continued in their rhythms, but the nonchalance was studied now; they kept a furtive eye on one another—Onions could follow the boy's big white hat—subconsciously gauging the other's secretive mission without the slightest desire to know what it was.

They paused to look at a blackeyed Susan or turned to watch a hawk glide over the bluffs. In ten minutes they came together and both looked up with formal faked surprise and called hello, moved in closer and chatted of casual public things for a few moments, then moved on their respective ways. Onions stopped seconds later and turned around to holler: "I'm going to marry your sister."

*****

Old Henry was painting his 300th August sunset, laying on his favorite orange with loving strokes, the orange with a healthy jot of turmeric in it. He sang as he worked: "Fry me a liver, fry me a liver— I fried a liver over you." And then he saw the head come bobbing down the river, a turnip-white relic of a head with the dour expression of a much-put-upon medieval saint. Henry walked over to look as it nodded in the river grasses. "Is that you? Is it you in the bulrushes, Moses?" He wedged it securely against the riverbank with the legs of his easel and hurried up to the house.

"Margaret," he yelled to his wife, "we had better call the Department of Decapitation!"

*****

The wedding feast—Eliza had driven alone up to see Beatrice Voice one evening, found her dozing on her porch: "Should I marry Robert Onions?" "Sure you should. Marry him! God bless you! He's only seventy years old. He's a good man. Just hide his car keys and tie his ballocks to the bedpost every night. You'll do just fine!"—the wedding feast a week later was about the last of the young people's mime. Whatever thought it up and blew it in was sailing on.

The celebrants stood around the tables in Onions's yard on the knoll above the river. The old gathered on one side in the shade of the house, the young congregated on the other, and they all wore their nearly identical clothing one final time. The narrow Model-T shoes with buffalo burrs in their laces, the shawls and striped suspenders. Only the middle-aged guests, the generation in between, looked oddly out of order and uninformed in their polyester shirts and denims, appeared flatfooted, even inadequate in the hilltop sun.

They ate cake and ice cream and Beatrice was rolling her blind eyes, telling woolly stories of insatiable old men after dark. Late afternoon, Onions came from the house with a cluster of helium balloons and after a brief word set them loose by the river.

"We're going airborne."

Half an hour later, Henry, bent beside his easel, saw them float over high above the Missouri, cheery little specks he believed for a moment were creatures of his own playing tag across his cornea, then recognized as minor foreign bodies in the vista, transient flecks strayed in from some unknown upstream palette, and paused to blow his nose and retie his shoes until they passed from sight.